Sins

Of The

City

Laura Wilkinson

DEDICATION

I want to thank my husband for always challenging me and supporting me in everything I do. I would also like to thank Maw & Deedah for being my beta readers on my first book.

TABLE OF CONTENTS

Chapter 1

A Broken Halo

Seraphiel stood on the ledge of the crumbling rooftop, her silver hair catching the faint glow of the Moonlight. Her wings, once radiant and flawless, were now streaked with ashen silver, a stark reminder of her fall from grace. The city below pulsed with life, its streets a maze of neon lights and shadows, A fitting backdrop for the angel who walked the fine line between divine purpose and mortal frailty. Eterna was indeed in full force tonight.

She had not asked for redemption – it had been imposed upon her. "Protect humanity," the voice of the archangel Michael had thundered when the decree was handed down. "Redeem yourself through their salvation." The irony of it did not escape her. She had fallen for defying the command to remain uninvolved, her compassion for the fragile lives of mortals deemed a betrayal. And now, her punishment was to guard those very lives.

Seraphiel adjusted the battered leather jacket she had taken to wearing, a strange comfort in its mortal texture. Beneath it, the faint shimmer of her celestial form still glowed, though dimly. Her task tonight was clear: a child, a boy not older than seven, was marked for death by the actions of a desperate man. She had seen his face in her visions – sunken eyes, trembling hands, the weight of debt driving him to an unspeakable act.

She dropped from the rooftop, her boots landing silently in the alley below. Eterna felt alive around her, but it was a different kind of life than the celestial choirs she had once known. Here, life was chaotic, messy, and filled with pain – and yet, it stirred something in her. She moved through the shadows, her senses heightened to the faint hum of danger, until she saw him: the man, clutching a pistol, pacing back and forth outside a dingy tenement.

The boy was inside, Seraphiel knew, asleep and unaware of the fragile thread holding his life together. The man muttered to himself, his breath fogging in the cold night air. Guilt warred with desperation in his eyes, and Seraphiel felt a pang in her chest. He wasn't evil, just broken. Like so many others.

She stepped into the dim light of the flickering street lamp, her wings tucked tightly against her back. "It doesn't have to be this way," she said, her voice soft but firm.

The man startled, turning to her with the wild–eyed panic of a cornered animal. "Who – what are you?"

"Someone who knows what you're about to do." She held his gaze, her own filled with a strange mix of sorrow and authority. "And someone who knows why."

His grip tightened on the pistol. "I don't have a choice."

"There's always a choice," She said, stepping closer. Her presence seemed to calm him, though he didn't lower his weapon. "You think ending his life will solve your problems, but it won't. It'll only destroy what little soul you have left."

The man's eyes brimmed with tears. "I'm out of time. The debt collectors – they'll kill me and my family."

Seraphiel felt the weight of his despair, the crushing inevitability of his circumstances. She had seen this before, countless times, in numerous lives. But the role wasn't to intervene directly – not anymore. Not unless she wanted to fall further. Instead, she reached out a hand, letting her celestial energy pulse faintly.

"You can't undo what's been done, but you can choose a different path," she said. Her voice carried a strange resonance, A whisper of the divine power she still held. "Let me help you. There's still hope."

The man stared at her, his hands trembling. Slowly, painfully, he lowered the gun. "I don't know what to do."

Seraphiel took the weapon from him, her touch gentle. "Start by going home to your family. Tell them the truth. It won't be easy, but it's better than this."

He nodded, his shoulder sagging as the weight of his decision sank in. Without another word, he turned and disappeared into the night, leaving Seraphiel alone in the silence of the alley.

She exhaled slowly, her wings unfurling slightly. The boy was safe, for now. But the man's troubles weren't over, and neither were hers. She had done what she could, but the lines between divine purpose and mortal interference blurred with every choice she made. Redemption was a heavy burden, and one she wasn't sure she deserved.

As she walked back into the shadows, Seraphiel whispered a quiet prayer, not to the Heavens she had once served, but to the fragile souls she now protected. Perhaps, in saving them, she could one day save herself.

Seraphiel knew why she had fallen from Heaven. It was because of her refusal to abide by one of the most sacred laws of the celestial order: non-intervention in mortal affairs. In the celestial hierarchy, angels were forbidden to interfere directly with human lives unless commanded by the divine. Mortals, after all, were granted free will, and angels were meant to guide subtly, not control outcomes.

But Seraphiel's heart had always been drawn to humanity's fragility and resilience. Unlike many of her brethren, who viewed mortals with detached reverence or even disdain, she saw their struggles as something sacred-a reflection of the divine itself. Over the centuries, she had grown increasingly frustrated with the suffering she witnessed: famine, war, disease, and despair. To her, standing by in silence while innocence suffered felt like a betrayal of her purpose as an angel. Her breaking point came during a great plague that swept across a kingdom. Seraphiel, then a high-ranking angel of compassion, was tasked with offering comfort to the souls of the dying. But when she saw the suffering of children, their lives extinguished before they had truly begun, she could no longer remain passive. Against direct orders, she descended to earth, manifesting her celestial power to heal the sick and save the dying. Villages were restored, lives prolonged, and hope rekindled where there had been none.

However, her actions did not go unnoticed. To mortals, she became a miracle, but to the celestial order, she had committed a grievous act of defiance. Her intervention disrupted the balance of fate and free will, and worse, her compassion, though born of purity, threatened the grand design. Seraphiel was summoned before the council of archangels, where her disobedience was judged harshly.

"I acted out of love," she had argued, her voice steady despite the weight of the accusations. "Is that not what we are meant to embody?"

But love, they reminded her, was not hers to give unconditionally. Her role was to serve the will of the divine, not to act on her own.

Michael, the commander of Heaven's armies, had been the one to cast the final sentence. Though there was sorrow in his voice, there was no hesitation. "You are allowed in your heart to overrule your duty, Seraphiel. That is the sin of pride, cloaked in the guise of mercy. You must bear the consequences."

With those words, her wings were marked with a gray, her radiant aura dimmed, and the gates of Heaven closed to her. She was neither fully angel nor fully mortal but something in between —a fallen guardian, tasked with protecting the very beings she had sacrificed her place in the celestial order to save.

Her fall was not met with rage or bitterness, but with an aching sense of loss. She had believed her actions were righteous, yet the weight of her punishment revealed the enormity of her defiance.

Now, as she roamed the mortal world, Seraphiel carried the constant burden of guilt, wondering if she had truly done what was right or if her pride had blinded her to a greater truth.

As Seraphiel rounded the corner to her apartment building, her wings started to tingle. She knew something wasn't right. A quick glance around and her attention was immediately drawn to the glow of fire and the smell of smoke in the air. In the smoldering wreckage of a tenement building, a fire had consumed the structure, spreading through the block like a vengeful wildfire. It appeared that a local gang had set the blaze in retaliation against those who dared to resist their extortion racket. Seraphiel had arrived just in time to shield a few trapped families from the falling debris, using the remnants of her celestial power to guide them to safety. By the time she had emerged from the ruined structure, her energy was spent, and the soot – covered angel was a faint shadow

of the divine figure she had once been. That's when Captain Naomi Blackwood appeared.

The captain, newly promoted to lead the city's special response task force, had been dispatched to the scene to manage the fallout of the fire. She was in her element – issuing commands, coordinating emergency services, and directing the first responders with practiced precision. Seraphiel, standing apart from the chaos, watched her with quiet fascination. There was something magnetic about Captain Blackwood's presence, a commanding force that seemed to draw people to her even amid calamity.

Naomi was less enchanted by the figure standing at the edge of the scene. The strange woman's signed leather jacket and ash–streaked silver hair caught her eye, as did her unearthly stillness. Naomi had seen plenty of people who lingered at the edges of tragedy–gawkers, opportunists, and survivors alike – but something about this one set her instincts on edge.

"You," Naomi called out as she approached, her tone sharp and authoritative. "What are you doing here? Are you hurt?"

Seraphiel turned to face her, meeting Naomi's piercing gaze with a calmness that seemed almost unnatural. "No, I'm fine."

Naomi frowned. "You were inside, weren't you? I saw you come out before the first responders. Who are you? And don't tell me you're just a concerned citizen."

For a moment, Seraphiel considered her answer. She wasn't sure why, but this mortal's intensity demanded honesty. "My name is Seraphiel," she said finally. I was helping."

Naomi's eyes narrowed. "Helping how? People were saying something about a 'bright figure' in the building. You wouldn't happen to know anything about that, would you?"

Seraphiel remained silent, her expression unreadable, which only fueled Naomi's suspicions. The Captain crossed her arms.

"Look, I don't know who or what you are, but this city has enough problems without vigilantes playing hero. If you're going to operate in my city, I need answers."

"Your city?" Seraphiel asked, a faint note of curiosity in her otherwise steady tone.

"Yes," Naomi said firmly. "I'm Captain Naomi Blackwood. And whoever or whatever you are, you're stepping into a world that doesn't take kindly to loose cannons."

Seraphiel tilted her head, a faint glimmer of amusement in her otherwise somber eyes. "And what would you do if I were a loose cannon, Captain Blackwood?"

Naomi took a step closer, her jaw tightening. "I'd figure out whether you're an ally or a threat. Fast."

Seraphiel studied her for a long moment, then let out a quiet sigh. "I am not your enemy, Captain. I have no interest in disrupting your… territory. But things are happening in this city that you can't handle alone."

Naomi bristled at the implication. "And you think you can?"

Seraphiel nodded. "I know I can. If you'll let me."

Naomi stared at her, weighing the words carefully. There was something about Seraphiel —something both unnerving and compelling. She didn't trust her, not yet, but there was an undeniable sincerity in her voice. And, as much as she hated to admit it, Naomi knew her city was teetering on the edge of collapse. Help, even from an unknown source, might be exactly what she needed.

"Fine," Naomi said, at last, her voice grudging. "But if you're going to be involved, you're going to do it my way. No disappearing into the shadows, no breaking the law, and no 'bright figure' nonsense. We do this by the book. Got it?"

Seraphiel's Lips curled into the faintest hint of a smile. "Understood."

It was a tenacious truce, but it was enough. From that moment, Naomi and Seraphiel became unlikely partners, each navigating their burdens while learning to trust one another. For Naomi, Seraphiel was an enigma – a puzzle she couldn't quite solve. For Seraphiel, Naomi was a reminder of why she had fallen in the first place: Humanity's stubborn, beautiful refusal to give up, even in the face of impossible odds.

Just then, Naomi's radio went off. She was being summoned to an even darker part of the city. There had been a gruesome murder. She waved at two other officers & glanced at Seraphiel as she turned toward her car. "You coming?"

Chapter 2

A Hunger for Justice

The moon hung low over the expansive city of Eterna, its pale light casting long shadows across the cobblestone streets. In the labyrinth of alleys that went through the city's forgotten districts, Lucian moved with the silent grace of a predator, his black coat trailing behind him like a spectre. To most, he was a myth – an immortal relic of darker days. But to those who trafficked in secrets and lies, he was a name whispered in fear: an informant, a manipulator, a survivor, a vampire.

Tonight, however, Lucian was being hunted.

The accusations had come swiftly and loudly, louder than any secret in Eterna's deep underbelly should have been. A high–ranking noble Judge was found dead in his chambers at the Golden Spire-Eclipse Hall, his body drained of blood. The work of a vampire, they claimed, and Lucian's name was the one spat from every frightened tongue.

He cursed softly as he vaulted over a little wall, landing noiselessly in the shadows of a decaying warehouse. Lucian hadn't tasted noble blood in over a century —it was far too conspicuous, far too dangerous —but truth rarely mattered when fear took root. Someone wanted him silenced, and framing him for murder was an effective way to do it.

"You're Faster than I expected," a voice called from the darkness, sharp and commanding.

Lucian froze, his golden eyes narrowing as Captain Naomi Blackwood stepped into view, flanked by two armed officers and an Angel. Her black leather coat and gleaming Eterna guard insignia reflected the moonlight, but it was her piercing gaze that held his attention. Naomi Blackwood was no stranger to the supernatural; she was known for her unflinching resolve when dealing with creatures that lurked beyond humanity's reach. The creatures that went bump in the night knew that she bumped back.

"Captain Blackwood," Lucian said evenly, brushing the dust from his coat. "If you're here to drag me to a holding cell, you'll find I am not inclined to cooperate tonight." He made an uneasy nod to Seraphiel.

Naomi crossed her arms, her dark eyes studying him like a hawk sizing up its prey. "If I thought you were guilty, you'd already be chained in silver and halfway to the Spire dungeons," she said. "But we both know you didn't kill Lord Merrick."

Lucian's lips curved into a faint smile. "How refreshingly reasonable. And here I thought the guard would prefer to see me burned at the stake."

"Don't tempt me," Naomi replied coolly. "You're not exactly a model citizen, Lucian. But you don't make mistakes like this – too messy, too brazen. Whoever killed Merrick wants us chasing you instead of them. I don't have time for wild goose chases."

Lucian's amusement flickered. He stepped closer, his voice dropping to a dangerous murmur. "If you're so convinced of my innocence, why bring an entourage that includes the Angel? Or is this just your way of reminding me how expendable I am?" Lucian and Seraphiel had had regular run-ins with each other in the past. Every creature of the night had heard of the fallen angel. Even though her halo was not as bright as it once was, she was still a force to be reckoned with and one that most supernatural beings did not want to cross paths with.

Naomi didn't flinch. "I'm not here to arrest you, Lucian. I'm here to offer you a chance to clear your name –and prove you're more useful to me alive than dead."

The Vampire tilted his head, intrigued despite himself. "You have my attention. Do go on."

She glanced at her officers, motioning for them to stay back. When she spoke again, Seraphiel was still at her side. Her tone was lower, almost conspiratorial. "Merrick wasn't just any notable. He was funding a secret project for the council – something big, something dangerous. I need a team who can navigate Eterna's shadows, people who know where the bodies are buried."

Lucian raised an eyebrow. "And you think I can be part of this team?"

"You've spent centuries learning every dirty secret in the city," Naomi said. "If anyone can find the truth, it's you. Help me, and I'll make sure the council knows you were framed. Refuse, and I can't promise they won't send the whole guard after you."

Lucian's eyes gleamed with a mix of amusement and calculation. "A tempting offer, Captain. But working with the guard? That's a bit… unorthodox for someone in my position." He gave a slight glance at Seraphiel. She held his glance for a few seconds, "Do you have something better going on in your life?" she asked with a shrug.

"Desperate times," Naomi said bluntly. "We both know whoever did this isn't going to stop with Merrick. They will come for you next. This is your chance to get ahead of them – and maybe even come out of it alive."

The silence stretched between them, heavy with unspoken truths. Lucian could hear the steady beat of Naomi's heart, the faint rustle of her officers shifting their weight, and the faint hum of Seraphiel's halo. He hated being cornered and hated the feeling of someone else pulling the strings. But Naomi was right about one thing: if he didn't act, the hunters would catch up to him eventually.

Finally, he exhaled, a soft chuckle escaping his lips. "Fine. I'll play your little game, Captain.

But make no mistake –if this goes sideways, I'll disappear faster than your guards can draw their weapons."

Naomi allowed herself a faint smile. "Then let's make sure it doesn't go sideways."

As they stepped into the night together, an unlikely alliance forged in the shadows, Lucian couldn't shake the feeling that this was only the beginning. Eterna's secrets ran deep, and if someone had gone to such lengths to frame him, it meant the truth was far darker than he'd imagined. And for the first time in centuries, Lucian wasn't sure he would survive what was coming.

Centuries ago, long before Eterna's towering spires and scattered alleys were even a dream, Lucian was a mortal Man, a noble–born son in the kingdom of Drevoria. As the second son of Duke Adrastos Valerian, Lucian was raised in the shadow of his older brother, a dutiful heir who embodied every virtue expected of their lineage. Lucian, by contrast, was a restless soul, drawn to the freedom of the night and the mysteries that lay beyond the rigid confines of court life.

It was in his twenty–fourth year that his life took a fateful turn. During a clandestine hunting trip with companions who sought more thrill than prey, Lucian ventured into a forbidden stretch of forest. There, under a blood moon, he encountered a creature of natural beauty and unspeakable hunger –a vampire named Kaelith. She seduced him with whispered promises of eternal freedom, of escape from the chains of mortality and obligation. Blinded by arrogance and curiosity, Lucian succumbed.

The transformation was agony, a violent ripping of his soul from his mortal body. When he woke, Kaelith was gone, leaving him alone to face the monstrous hunger that consumed him. He returned to his family estate only to find himself unable to resist the pull of their blood. In his frenzy, Lucian attacked his brother, and though he stopped short of killing him, the act branded him as a monster. He fled into the night, the weight of his sin driving him far from the life he once knew.

For the next two centuries, Lucian wandered across continents, learning to survive in the shadows. He became a thief, an assassin, and sometimes a reluctant savior, his existence a mosaic of contradictions. But his immortality came with a curse: the further he delved into his vampiric nature, the more he lost touch with his humanity. He avoided forming attachments, knowing they would end in either betrayal or death.

By the time he reached Eterna –then a burgeoning trade city perched on the edge of a vast sea – Lucian had shed his noble past entirely. He arrived under the cover of night, drawn by whispers of its thriving underworld and the anonymity its chaos could provide. The city's dark alleys and gilded halls were a perfect hunting ground, but Lucian quickly realized Eterna was no ordinary city. Its veins pulsed with ancient power, its rulers dabbling in magics they barely understood.

At first, Lucian sought only to survive, feeding discreetly and taking refuge in the city's forgotten corners. But over time, he found himself entangled in Eterna's shadowy politics. Secrets were currency in Eterna, and few were better at uncovering them than an immortal predator who could hear whispers through walls and charm the truth from the most guarded lips.

Lucian became a broker of information, a puppet master pulling strings from the fringes. He struck deals with crime lords, merchants, and even members of the city's ruling council, always keeping just enough distance to avoid becoming a target. His reputation grew, and with it came a strange kind of stability. For the first time in centuries, Lucian wasn't running.

But Eterna's darkness had a way of claiming those who lingered too long. Despite his careful maneuvering, Lucian couldn't avoid entanglement with the city's more profound mysteries. He uncovered fragments of an ancient prophecy that hinted at a war between mortals and immortals, with Eterna at its heart. Though he dismissed it as superstition, the prophecy haunted him, a reminder that even eternity could end.

Lucian stayed in Eterna not because he trusted its people, but because the city felt like a mirror of himself – beautiful on the surface, but rotten at its core. He told himself he didn't care about its fate, that he was only a player in its endless game of shadows. But somewhere in the depths of his undead heart, Lucian wondered if this cursed city was the only home he'd ever truly have.

When he was rumored to have murdered Lord Merrick, it wasn't just his life at stake –It was the fragile balance of power he had spent centuries maintaining. What Naomi was offering him was a chance to clear his name, and Lucian knew he had to accept.

Not because he wanted redemption, but because he refused to let anyone take Eterna away from him.

After all, Lucian was as much a part of Eterna as the city's crumbling stones and whispered secrets. And if someone wanted to destroy him, they'd have to destroy the city first.

Chapter 3

The Beast Within

The roar of the crowd rose and fell in waves, vibrating through the air like a living thing. The underground cage was illuminated by dim, flickering light, creating shadows. He was panting, his eyes locked onto his opponent – a towering brute who dwarfed him by a good 50 pounds. Yet it wasn't the size that determined dominance in the cage. It was ferocity, and Cassian had it in spades.

The bell rang, and the large man charged forward, his fists swinging like wrecking balls. Cassian didn't move, not immediately. He stood there, eerily calm, like a predator waiting for the perfect moment to strike. When the first punch came, Cassian ducked under it with an almost animalistic fluidity. His counterattack was vicious – a sharp elbow to the ribs followed by a hook to the jaw that sent his opponent stumbling.

The crowd erupted, some in awe, others in fear. They'd seen fights before, but none like this. Cassian wasn't just fighting to win; he was venting something dark, something that ran deeper than the sport of it. His strikes were brutal, precise, and unrelenting. His opponent never had a chance.

By the time the fight ended, the man lay crumpled on the mat, groaning in agony, while Cassian stood over him, his chest glistening with sweat and his eyes glowing faintly in the dim light. The crowd's cheers turned hesitant, uncertain. There was something about him that unnerved even the most hardened spectators. They could sense it –the barely contained beast beneath his skin.

Cassian climbed out of the cage, brushing past a few hesitant admirers who reached for him, their praise dying in their throats at his glower. He grabbed a towel, wiping the blood from his knuckles as he headed for the exit. The flight was over, and so was his brief reprieve from the restless anger that clawed at his insides.

That's when he saw them.

Three figures waited near the corridor that led to the locker rooms. Captain Blackwood, tall and imposing in her black coat, flanked by two others. Lucian, with his sharp features and cool, calculating gaze, and Seraphiel, who stood slightly apart, her silver hair catching the dim light like a halo. It was her gaze that locked onto Cassian first, piercing, knowing.

He stopped, instinctively bristling. Something about Seraphiel set him on edge, as though she could see straight through the tough exterior he worked so hard to maintain.

"Cassian," Naomi greeted, her deep voice carrying a weight of authority. "We need to talk."

"I'm not interested," Cassian muttered, shouldering past them.

Seraphiel stepped into his path, her eyes narrowing. "You should be." Her voice was calm but firm, with an edge that hinted at an unshakable confidence. "I can feel it – your nature. You're barely holding it together."

Cassian's lips curled in a sneer. "Stay out of my head, angel. "

Lucian raised an eyebrow, amused. "You should listen to her, wolf. She's rarely wrong about these things."

"I said, I'm not interested," Cassian growled, the sound low and guttural, his anger flaring. "Whatever you're selling, I'm not buying."

"That's not what this is," Naomi cut in, her voice sharper now. "We're offering you a chance – an opportunity to make amends for your past."

Cassian froze, his jaw tightening. He didn't respond, but the flicker of guilt in his eyes was enough for Naomi to press on.

"We know about the gangs. The fights. The destruction you've left in your wake." Naomi's tone softened, just enough to cut through Cassian's defenses. "You can't change what you've done, but you can decide what kind of man – or wolf – you want to be moving forward."

Cassian's hands clenched into fists at his sides. The weight of his past felt heavier than ever, pressing down on him like a stone.

He didn't trust them – not yet – but something about Naomi's words lingered.

"Get out of my way," he muttered, pushing past them and disappearing into the locker rooms.

The next fight was different.

The moon was almost full, its pull thrumming through Cassian's veins like a drug. He stood in the cage again, his opponent forgotten, the world around him a blur. The rage was harder to contain this time, his wolf clawing to get free. His nails sharpened, his eyes glowed amber, and a low growl escaped his throat.

The crowd fell silent, their excitement shifting to fear.

And then she was there.

Seraphiel stood at the edge of the cage, her calm presence cutting through the chaos like a blade. She didn't speak, didn't try to stop him. She simply stood there, her steady gaze locking onto his.

Cassian's transformation faltered, the beast inside recoiling at her unflinching calm. Slowly, painfully, he forced himself back, his claws retracting, his breathing evening out. When he finally looked up, Seraphiel was still standing there, her expression unreadable.

"You don't run," he rasped, his voice raw with emotion.

"No," she replied simply. "And neither should you."

For the first time in years, Cassian felt the rage inside him settle, if only for a moment. And in that moment, he realized something he hadn't allowed himself to believe in a long time.

Maybe redemption wasn't entirely out of reach.

Cassian was taken back to a past life where he was once the hammer of the Crimson Howl Pack, a feared and ruthless enforcer who carried out the dirty work that kept his pack at the top of the food chain. For years, he thrived in their brutal, lawless world. His strength, combat skill, and unrelenting rage made him a valuable asset, and he quickly climbed the ranks, becoming the pack leader's most trusted weapon. But the price of loyalty was steep, and each mission etched deeper scars into his soul.

The turning point came during what was supposed to be a routine operation – an ambush on a rival pack that had encroached on Crimson Howl territory. Cassian had been ordered to lead the pack, to strike fast, and leave no survivors. He followed orders without hesitation; it was what he'd always done. But things spiraled out of control. The rival pack hadn't been alone – there were civilians there, too, humans caught in the crossfire.

By the time the dust settled, the ground was soaked in blood, and the air was filled with the cries of the wounded and dying. Cassian found himself standing in the center of the carnage, his hands stained crimson. The faces of those who had died by his claws haunted him, their expressions of terror seared into his mind.

For the first time, Cassian questioned everything – the pack, his loyalty, and, most of all, himself. The Crimson Howl's leader, a cold and calculating alpha named Draven Nightflame, dismissed the collateral damage as a necessary cost of war. But Cassian couldn't. The guilt gnawed at him, and the anger he had once directed outward began to turn inward, threatening to consume him.

Unable to live with what he had done, Cassian abandoned the pack, disappearing into the shadows of Eterna. His departure wasn't without consequence – Draven branded him a traitor, putting a bounty on his head that ensured he could never truly rest. For years, Cassian tried to suppress the beast inside him, the anger and violence that had defined his life. He worked odd jobs, kept to himself, and avoided the full moons as best he could. But the rage never left, bubbling beneath the surface, ready to erupt at the slightest provocation.

Eterna's underground fight clubs became both a refuge and a curse. The cage offered him a place to vent his anger, to unleash the beast in a controlled environment. But each fight left him closer to the edge, the line between man and wolf growing thinner with every battle. The spectators feared him, sensing the barely–contained fury that made him as dangerous outside the cage as he was within it.

Cassian tried to convince himself that he was in control, that he could keep the wolf on a leash. But deep down, he knew the truth. He wasn't running from the Crimson Howl or the bounty hunters Draven sent after him. He was running from himself, from the monster he had become and the lives he had destroyed.

When Naomi and Seraphiel approached him, Cassian was ready to brush them off like everyone else. But Naomi's words struck a nerve, dredging up memories he had spent years trying to bury. The Captain spoke with redemption, of using his strength to make amends for the blood on his hands. It wasn't an easy sell – Cassian didn't believe he deserved redemption. But the thought of channeling his rage into something other than destruction was enough to give him pause.

Now, caught between his violent past and an uncertain future, Cassian walked like a razor's edge. He didn't trust easily, and he wasn't sure he could ever fully escape the shadow of the Crimson Howl. But part of him hoped that by fighting alongside Blackwood's team, by confronting the monsters outside and within, he might finally find a way to tame the beast – and maybe, a measure of peace.

Cassian suddenly felt someone rubbing his shoulder. It was her. She was not scared of him in the least. "Come on," Seraphiel whispered. "You're too good for this kind of life anymore." As she brought him back to reality, Cassian felt hopeful for the first time in a long time. Maybe this was actually his chance for redemption. As Cassian followed her out of the ring and to the others, Seraphiel formally introduced herself. "My name is Seraphiel, but you can call me Sera. We have one more stop to make, and we're going to need you at one hundred percent."

Chapter 4

Secrets In The Smoke

Rowan leaned against the counter of her magic shop, a chipped porcelain teacup in one hand and a battered grimoire in the other. The shop, tucked away in the shadowy corners of the city, was a labyrinth of shelves sagging under the weight of dusty tomes, jars of pickled herbs, and glittering talismans. Candles flickered in the sconces mounted on exposed brick walls, casting long shadows that danced like restless spirits. It was a place of secrets, and Rowan had plenty of her own.

The soft chime of the shop's bell pulled her from her reading. She set the grimoire aside, her green eyes narrowing as a figure stepped through the threshold. The man was wiry, with sharp features and a nervous energy that clung to him like a second skin. His gaze darted around the shop before settling on Rowan.

"You Rowan?" he asked, his voice low and jittery.

She tilted her head, feigning disinterest. "Depends on who's asking."

"I'm… in need of something specific." He glanced over his shoulder, as if expecting to find someone tailing him. "A hex. A strong one."

Rowan's expression hardened. "You've got the wrong place. I don't deal in that kind of magic anymore."

The man leaned closer, his voice dropping to a conspiratorial whisper. "I'm willing to pay handsomely. Gold. Spelled sigils. Whatever you want."

"Not interested," she replied, turning back to her book. But he wasn't deterred.

"I have this," he said, reaching into his coat and producing a small, intricate box. He opened it just enough for Rowan to glimpse the artifact inside: a shard of gleaming obsidian, etched with faint runes that pulsed with an otherworldly light.

Rowan's breath caught in her throat. An Aether Shard. Rare, potent, and nearly impossible to find. The kind of artifact witches like her could only dream of owning.

She clenched her jaw, fighting the temptation that clawed at her resolve. "That's not for a hex," she said. "That's for the binding magic. Whoever gave that to you is either a fool or has a death wish."

The man's smile was thin, all teeth and no worth. "Doesn't matter. Do we have a deal?"

Rowan hesitated, her fingers brushing the edge of the counter. She's sworn to keep her nose clean, but the shard… The power it contained could amplify her abilities in ways she hadn't dared to imagine. It wasn't just a temptation – it was an opportunity.

"Fine," she said, taking the shard, her voice sharp with irritation.

As she began gathering the components for the hex, the tension in the room thickened. She muttered incantations under her breath, her hands moving with practiced precision. The magic thrummed in the air, dark and electric.

Just as she reached the final step, the shop door burst open with a crash. Rowan spun around, her heart leaping into her throat as four figures stormed inside. At the head of the group was Captain Naomi Blackwood, her commanding presence impossible to ignore. She stepped forward, flanked by her task force: Lucian, the brooding enforcer; Sera, a sharp-eyed angel; and Cassian, a towering shifter with an ever-present scowl.

"Rowan Hawthorne," Naomi said, her raspy voice laced with authority. "Caught red-handed, I see."

Rowan's pulse quickened as she raised her hands, the partially completed hex still glowing in her grasp. "Captain Blackwood. To what do I owe the pleasure?"

"Save it," she snapped. "We've been watching you for weeks. Selling illegal magic and consorting with criminals. And now this?" She gestured to the customer, who was already trying to slink toward the exit before Lucian blocked his path.

Rowan forced a smirk, though her mind raced for an escape. "I'm a simple shopkeeper. No laws against selling herbs and charms."

Don't play coy," Naomi said, stepping closer. Her dark eyes locked onto Rowan's, unyielding. "You have two choices: face incarceration for your… entrepreneurial endeavors, or join my task force. We need someone with your particular skill set."

Rowan's smirk faltered. "You're joking."

"Do I look like I'm joking?" Naomi's tone left no room for argument. "We're dealing with a surge of supernatural crime cases only someone like this team can crack. You help us, or you rot in a cell. Simple as that."

The shop was silent except for the faint crackle of magic still hanging in the air. Rowan's gaze flicked to the Aether Shard she had stashed on a nearby shelf, then to the task force, weighing her options. She hated the idea of being under Naomi's thumb, but prison wasn't exactly appealing either. Besides, part of her knew she was right. Her magic, as messy and dangerous as it was, could make a difference.

"Fine," she said, lowering her hands. "But don't expect me to like it." Naomi gave a curt nod. "Welcome to the team, Hawthorne. Try not to make me regret this."

As the task force escorted her out of the shop, Rowan glanced over her shoulder at the Aether Shard. It gleamed on the shelf, a promise of power left behind. She'd chosen survival over temptation - for now. But Rowan knew better than anyone that every choice came with a price.

Rowan Hawthorne's journey to the city of Eterna was one of survival, exile, and reluctant reinvention. Born into a powerful coven in the remote mist-shrouded forests of Oakspire Hollow, Rowan's early life was steeped in magic. Her family's magic was ancient and respected, their legacy one of guardianship over the natural and supernatural balance. But the legacy came with rules, strict ones, and Rowan had always been terrible at following them.

Her troubles began when she was barely out of her teens. Brash, clever, and craving independence, Rowan dabbled in the forbidden magic: blood spells, hexes, and shadowcraft. These practices were deemed too dangerous and volatile, even for her gifted family. Rowan justified it as a means to understand magic's full potential, but in truth, she was chasing power and the thrill of the unknown.

Her defiance came to a head when a summoning spell went catastrophically wrong. The entity she called forth escaped her control, wreaking havoc in their village and leaving scars that would never fully heal. Though Rowan ultimately banished the creature, the damage was done. Her coven, fearful and furious, branded her reckless and dangerous. Rather than outright execution-a fate she narrowly avoided-they cast her out, severing her ties to the coven and banishing her from Oakspire Hollow.

Alone and untethered, Rowan wandered for years, making a living on the fringes of society. She became a shadow in the magical underworld, using her skills for less-than-reputable clients. For a while, she thrived in the chaos. She was good at what she did-too good. Her reputation as a criminal witch grew, and with it came enemies.

One of those enemies eventually set her up. A betrayal by someone she trusted left her on the run, fleeing from the bounty hunters and magical enforcers alike. It was desperation that brought her to Eterna, which was known as a hub of supernatural trade and politics. The city's labyrinthine alleys and dense population made it the perfect place to disappear.

In Eterna, Rowan reinvented herself as the owner of The Hawthorne Bazaar, a tiny, unassuming magic shop tucked into the edges of the Old Quarter. To the casual observer, she was just another purveyor of charms and curiosities. But behind closed doors, Rowan operated in a gray area, occasionally selling illegal enchantments or handling jobs no one else would touch. She stayed under the radar, for the most part.

Still, the ghosts of her past lingered. Rowan's nights were haunted by the mistakes she couldn't undo, and though she told herself she didn't care, a part of her wanted to make amends. But her outlaw instincts always seemed to get the better of her, pulling her into trouble again and again.

Eterna became both her refuge and her cage. It was a city of second chances, but for Rowan, it felt like a place where she was forever balancing on the edge of ruin.

Until Captain Blackwood's task force stormed into her shop, Rowan believed she could keep skating by, one deal at a time.

But now, with the weight of the law hanging over her, she was forced to face the question she'd been avoiding for years: was redemption even possible for someone like her?

With Naomi's team in place, they headed to the Golden Spire-Eclipse Hall to start their investigation.

Chapter 5

Shadows Beneath the Spire

The condition inside Eclipse Hall was heavy, the golden spires catching rays of morning light, but failing to illuminate the shadows that clung to its grand chambers. Naomi strode into the murder scene, her boots clicking sharply against the marble floor. A noble judge, Lord Elric Merrick, lay sprawled across his opulent desk, his lifeless eyes staring into eternity. The air reeked of blood, ink, and a faint, acrid tang Naomi couldn't quite place.

Sera hovered just behind, her silver wings furled tightly against her back. Her grey hair shimmered faintly in the dim light, a stark contrast to the grim expression on her face.

Lucian was already there, his crimson eyes scanning the room with a predatory focus. "The wound isn't natural," he said, pointing to the jagged gash across the judge's chest. "This wasn't done with any human blade."

Cassian growled low in his throat as he crouched to sniff the blood pooling around the desk. "The scent is… It's not just human. There's something… ancient in it."

Rowan stepped forward, her emerald eyes narrowing as she examined the intricate symbols carved into the desk near the judge's hand. Her auburn hair seemed to spark with energy as she traced a finger over the marks. "This isn't a random killing," she murmured. "This is a ritual."

Naomi leaned over, her keen eyes studying the symbols. "What kind of ritual?"

Rowan hesitated, her voice laced with unease. "One that ties to the supernatural. "This symbol here–" she pointed to a sigil resembling a coiled serpent surrounded by flames– "is ancient. It's a binding sigil, meant to harness power. But it hasn't been used in centuries. Whoever did this knew exactly what they were doing."

"Which means," Lucian said, straightening, "this wasn't just an assassination. It was a message."

Sera's soft voice cut through the tension. "And the message is clear. No one, not even a noble judge, is safe from whoever–whatever–is behind this."

Naomi's jaw tightened. "We need answers, and we need them fast. I'm going to bet we can find some underground."

The trail of clues had led them to Shadowfalls. Hidden behind a dilapidated warehouse, the entrance was guarded by wards that Rowan dismantled with a whispered incantation. As they stepped inside, the world shifted. Shadowfalls was more than a market; it was a living, breathing nexus where the supernatural world revealed its unfiltered chaos. The hidden market that pulsed beneath the city like a secret heartbeat.

The air inside the extensive cavern felt alive with power, a hum that prickled against the skin and sent shivers down the spine. The ceiling stretched high above, threaded with glowing veins of bioluminescent moss that bathed the marketplace in a dim, eerie light. The underground expanse was a chaotic kaleidoscope of stalls, creatures, and wares. Supernaturals of all kinds bartered and argued in languages both ancient and new. The air was thick with the scent of magic, burning incense, and the metallic tang of blood. Vendors shouted their wares from shadowy alcoves; enchanted artifacts, forbidden tomes, blood vials, talismans pulsating faintly with trapped magic, and otherworldly creatures caged in wrought-iron stalls.

Naomi's team weaved through the bustling crowd. Creatures of all kinds–fae with glittering wings, shadowed wraiths, towering trolls, and others too strange to name–watched them with wary eyes. Conversations in ancient and gruff languages faded into silence as the task force passed.

"They don't trust us," Cassian muttered, his wolfish senses picking up every flicker of hostility.

"Good," Naomi said rudely, scanning the stalls. "I don't trust them either."

Lucian's expression darkened as he scanned the crowd. "Tensions are high. The factions are on edge."

"They've been on edge since the Accords were signed," Cassian said. "But this? This is worse."

Naomi's sharp gaze landed on a figure standing above the chaos. At the heart of Shadowfalls, on a raised dais, stood Astrion. She was a Luminarea, a vision of otherworldly power, her veins glowing faintly with molten light that pulsed in time with her heartbeat. Her eyes shimmered with an unsettling calm, a mix of Volcanic fury and Oracle wisdom. At some point centuries ago, an Etherean, made up of pure, glowing energy noticeably running through their veins and said to be born from the last breath of dying volcanoes, had fallen in love with an Oracle. Oracles were known to be brilliant, calm, and loving creatures that could see the threads of fate and weave them to change outcomes, but at a dire cost to their physical form.

"She's the one who runs this place," Rowan whispered. "If anyone knows about that symbol, it'll be her."

As they approached, the crowd parted, wary of the unlikely task force. Astrion turned her glowing gaze toward them, her lips curling into a knowing smile. "Captain Blackwood," she said, her voice smooth and resonant. "I've been expecting you."

Naomi's hand instinctively rested on the hilt of her sword. "Then you know why we're here."

"I do," Astrion said, descending the dais with an almost liquid grace. "You seek answers about the judge's murder. And about the sigil."

Rowan stepped forward, holding out a sketch of the symbol. "What do you know about this?"

Astrion's expression grew somber as she studied the sketch. "This is the mark of the Bound Flame," she said. "It's tied to an ancient pact, one that was forged long before your kind walked this earth. It binds power to those willing to pay the price."

"What kind of power?" Sera asked, her voice soft but firm.

"The kind that topple kingdoms and shatter the balance of the supernatural world," Astrion replied. Her glowing veins pulsed brighter. "And the kind of price that would make even the bravest soul think twice."

Naomi narrowed her eyes. "Who would use it now? And why?"

Astrion hesitated, a flicker of pain crossing her serene features. "The sigil hasn't been seen in centuries. Its use is forbidden, even among the most reckless. But if someone is wielding it now... They're trying to awaken something that should remain buried."

Cassian growled low in his throat. "And Shadow Falls? What's your role in all of this?"

Astrion's glowing eyes locked onto his. "I am the keeper of balance here, wolf. My market is a sanctuary, not a battlefield. But even I cannot stop the threads of fate from fraying."

Naomi's voice was steel. "Then help us. Give us a name, a lead – anything."

For a moment, Astrion said nothing, her gaze distant as though peering into the very fabric of destiny. Then she spoke, her voice heavy with foreboding. "Seek the Crimson Hollow. There, you will find the answers you seek – and the danger you fear."

The task force exchanged grim looks. The Crimson Hollow was a place whispered of in fear, a nexus of power and danger.

As they turned to leave, Astrion's voice stopped them. "Captain," she said, her glowing eyes locking onto Naomi's. "Be careful. The threads are unraveling, and the cost of failure will be more than you can bear."

Naomi's jaw tightened. "Then we won't fail."

And with that, they plunged deeper into the market, the weight of the mystery – and the fate of their world – pressing heavily on their shoulders. Rowan's sharp look landed on an inconspicuous stall tucked into a dark corner. Its vendor was cloaked in heavy, rune-stitched fabric, their face obscured by a mask that shimmered like liquid metal. On the stall's counter sat an assortment of strange items, including a cracked obsidian tablet inscribed with the same coiled serpent and flame symbol found on the judge's desk.

"This is it," Rowan said, gesturing for the others to follow her. She approached the vendor cautiously. "Where did you get this?"

The vendor tilted their head, their voice a low, musical hum. "The sigil of the Bound Flame… a relic of the old world, older than even this market. What is it to you, witch?"

"We're investigating a murder tied to this symbol," Naomi said bluntly, stepping beside Rowan. "What do you know about it?"

The vendor's laugh was unsettling, a brassy echo. "Many things are tied to that mark. Blood spilled. Power stolen. Deals struck in shadows."

"Stop playing games," Lucian growled, his eyes flashing. "Who's using it now?"

The vendor leaned forward, their masked face inches from Rowan's. "Follow ember trails," they whispered. "To the hollow, where the serpent sleeps."

Before Naomi could press further, the vendor snapped their fingers. A gust of icy wind extinguished the lanterns in the stall, and when the darkness cleared, the vendor—and the tablet—were gone.

"Damn it," Naomi swore. "They know something. Why disappear unless they're hiding it?"

"They pointed us toward the Crimson Hallow," Rowan said, her voice steady. "But why would they help us? It feels like a trap."

"It is a trap," Lucian said grimly. "But we don't have a choice."

Sera, ever perceptive, stopped at another stall run by a weather-beaten fae with spindly fingers and sharp, glittering eyes. The fae was meticulously organizing a collection of scrolls and ledgers bound in the enchanted leather.

"Information is my trade," the fae said smoothly, their voice like dry leaves rustling. "And for the right price, I might share something useful."

"What price?" Naomi asked warily.

"An ounce of trust," the fae replied with a sly grin. "And a drop of blood."

Cassian growled. "Not a chance."

Naomi cut him off with a gesture. She extended her hand, and the face produced a small, shimmering needle. With a sharp prick, the captain's blood glowed faintly as it fell into a waiting vial.

The fae smiled, licking their lips. "Generous. I'll make it worth your while."

They pulled out a ledger and opened it to a page marked with the Bound Flame sigil. The entries detailed trade transactions—names, dates, and items. One name stood out, repeated across several entries: Tavik Ryn.

"Who is Tavik Ryn?" Naomi demanded.

"A broker," the fae said. "One who deals in rare magic and forbidden rituals. He was here days ago, peddling rumors about Crimson Hollow. Said he had business there."

Sera frowned. "Do you know where we can find him?" The fae shrugged. "He travels light and fast, but if you're looking for him, I'd wager he's already deep in the hollow."

Naomi slammed the ledger shut. "Then that's where we're going."

As the group moved away from the fae's stall, Rowan's attention was caught by a glowing fragment of stone displayed at a stall toward the exit, adorned with runes. She paused, her hand covering it, her magic resonating with the artifact.

"What is this?" she asked the vendor, a gnarled old dwarf with a giant glint of greed in his eye.

"Fragment of a door," the dwarf said. "They say it belonged to the Hollow itself. Found it in the ruins of a sanctuary that went up in flames."

Rowan touched the fragment and gasped. Visions flickered before her eyes: a dark, cavernous space lit by flickering flames; shadows moving along the seal; and the faint sound of chanting.

She pulled back, her breath ragged. "It's connected to the sigil," she said. "The Hollow isn't just a place. It's a nexus of power."

"And danger," Sera added, her gaze solemn. "If the sigil originated there, we're walking into the heart of its creation."

By the time they left Shadowfalls, their path was clear. Tavik Ryn was the key, and Crimson Hollow was their destination. Yet the market's ominous atmosphere lingered, a warning they couldn't ignore.

As they ascended back into the city, Naomi glanced at her team. "We've got our lead, but keep your guard up. Shadowfalls gave us clues, but it also painted a target on our backs."

Cassian cracked his knuckles. "Let them come. I'll be ready."

Lucian smirked, but his eyes betrayed his unease. "Let's hope you're as ready as you think."

Sera spread her wings slightly, her calming presence easing the tension. "Whatever awaits us, we face it together."

Rowan held the stone fragment tightly, her thoughts already drifting to the visions she had seen. "The Hollow won't just test our strength," she said softly. "It will test our souls."

With the plan set, the task force headed to Crimson Hollow and the ancient secrets buried within, each member sharing and discussing the information and lore they had dealt with or heard of over the years.

Chapter 6

Crimson Hollow

Crimson Hollow was a place steeped in legend, fear, and the remnants of ancient, dark power. Hidden deep within a dense, foreboding forest, the Hollow had long been whispered about in the shadows of both human and supernatural communities. While few dared to venture near, those who did often spoke of its suffocating aura, unnatural silence, and the pervasive sense of being watched.

The origins of Crimson Hollow date back over a millennium, to a time when humans and supernaturals were locked in a bloody, unending conflict. According to fragmented texts and oral traditions, the Hollow was not always an epicenter of evil. Once, it was a sacred site where the veil between worlds was thin–a place where the energies of life, death, and magic converged in harmony. Witches and mystics called it the "Primal Crossroads" and used its natural power to heal, commune with spirits, and maintain a balance between realms.

However, the balance was shattered when a group of rogue mystics, later known as the Ascendants, discovered the site. They believed the Hollow's power could be harnessed not for balance, but for dominance. They sought to manipulate the veil between worlds, tearing it open to gain access to otherworldly forces.

Using forbidden blood magic, they conducted gruesome rituals, sacrificing both humans and supernaturals alike to channel the Hollow's energy for their own dark purposes.

These rituals corrupted the once-sacred site, turning the lush forest into a desolate, charred expanse. The natural magic of the Hollow twisted into something malevolent, and the veil between realms became unstable. The Ascendants' final, catastrophic ritual was halted by a coalition of witches, angels, and other supernaturals, but not before they succeeded in leaving a permanent scar on the land. The obelisk, marked with the serpent-and-flame sigil, was left behind as a tether to their power, ensuring the site's corruption remained.

Crimson Hollow now served as a center of power and danger, its purpose warped by centuries of dark magic. The site was now an intersection of energy lines, making it a focal point for supernatural energy. While it was inherently unstable and dangerous, it held immense potential for those willing to risk the consequences of tapping into it. Over the centuries, many had tried to use the Hollow's power for their own gain, but most had either perished or gone mad in the attempt.

For the Ascendants, Crimson Hollow was more than a source of power; it was a keystone in the apocalyptic plans. By fully reopening the veil between worlds, they aimed to summon ancient entities from beyond, beings of immense power and malice. These entities, bound to the Ascendants' will, would obliterate the fragile peace between humans and supernaturals, plunging the world into chaos and reshaping it in the Ascendants' vision.

To achieve this, the Ascendants must complete a series of rituals starting with Crimson Hollow, each tied to the serpent-and-flame-sigil. The sigil itself is a symbol of destruction and rebirth, representing the group's belief in tearing down the current world to create a new one under their control. The obelisk at the Hollow's center was both a focal point for their ritual and a gateway to the Void, the realm from which they draw their power.

Crimson Hollow was now rumored to be alive in its own way, feeding off fear and suffering. The forest surrounding it was unnaturally quiet, and those who approached often experienced hallucinations, whispers, and a growing sense of dread. Some legends claimed the spirits of those sacrificed by the Ascendants still wandered the Hollow, their anguished cries echoing through the mist.

The current condition of the site resulted from centuries of neglect, intermittent attempts to clean it, and ongoing interference by cults and dark practitioners. Despite its corruption, the Hollow retained traces of its original power, and some believed it could be restored to its sacred purpose. However, doing so would require unimaginable strength, both magical and supernatural.

For now, Crimson Hollow remained a forbidden place, its obelisk a dark monument to the Ascendants' arrogance and ambition. With the cult active once more, the Hollow was at the heart of their plans, poised to become the epicenter of an apocalyptic event that could change the world forever.

The air grew cooler as Naomi led her team along the winding path toward Crimson Hollow. The forest loomed thick and ominous around them, the bare branches clawing at the sky like skeletal fingers. Even the moonlight, pale and uncertain, seemed reluctant to pierce the heavy veil of the mist that clung to the ground. Naomi tightened her grip on the hilt of her sword, her sharp gaze scanning the shadowed terrain for any sign of danger.

"We're getting close," Rowan murmured, her voice low and laced with unease. The witch's emerald eyes glowed faintly in the dim light as she traced a rune in the air. The faint shimmer of magic revealed a path ahead, its edges marked with faint scorch marks and scattered bones. "The wards are old but strong. Whoever set these wanted to keep someone or something out."

"Or in," Cassian growled, his amber eyes gleaming with a feral light. The werewolf's hulking form moved with predatory grace, his senses on high alert. "This place stinks of blood and fear. Whatever's ahead isn't friendly."

"Fear is a natural response to the unknown," Sera said softly, her ashed wings glowing faintly in the dark. The angel's serene expression belied the tension in her posture, her fingers clutching the hilt of her golden blade. Her voice carried a hint of something unspoken, a weight she refused to share.

Lucian chuckled darkly, his fangs flashing as he walked beside her. "Fear is also a warning, dear angel. One that keeps us alive." His crimson eyes flicked toward Naomi. "Tell me, Captain, do you believe the whispers about Crimson Hollow? About what lies at its heart?"

The memory of the sigil – a coiled serpent surrounded by flames – flashed through her mind.

The crude carving had been discovered in the ruins of a human village, its inhabitants slaughtered in a manner that suggested both ritual and rage. Rowan had identified the symbol as ancient and powerful, tied to a group long thought extinct: the Ascendants.

"This place feels like a wound," Rowan said, her voice trembling as they reached the edge of the Hollow. The mist parted to reveal a vast expanse of scorched earth, dotted with jagged stone pillars. In the center of the clearing stood a black obelisk, its surface etched with the serpent sigil.

The team approached cautiously, the oppressive silence broken only by the crunch of their footsteps. Naomi raised a fist, signaling a halt. "Rowan, can you tell me what kind of magic we're dealing with?"

Rowan knelt, placing her hands on the ground. Her eyes rolled back as she muttered an incantation, her voice resonating with an otherworldly echo. Moments later, she gasped, recoiling as though burned.

"It's… It's tied to death and fire," she said, her voice asking. "Blood sacrifices. This place is a nexus of power, connected to the Ascendants. They're trying to –"

"To tear the veil between worlds," Sera interrupted, her voice sharper than usual. The angel's expression darkened as she stared at the obelisk." They seek to end the fragile peace between humans & supernaturals. Their goal is chaos, destruction, and dominance."

Naomi frowned, stepping closer to Sera. "You've known about this? How?"

Sera hesitated, her wings twitching. "There are things I cannot reveal, Captain. But I've… encountered the Ascendants before. They've existed for centuries, always lurking in the shadows, waiting for the right time to strike."

"And now they've chosen this time," Lucian said, his tone cold. "What do they hope to gain? Supernaturals and humans have barely avoided this war as it is."

"They believe they are the chosen ones," Sera replied, her voice bitter. "They think their chaos will lead to a new order, one where they reign supreme. The serpent and the flame – they symbolize rebirth through destruction." Cassian growled, his claws extending. "Then we destroy the obelisk and stop whatever they're planning."

"It's not that simple," Rowan warned. "Destroying it without understanding the magic could unleash whatever's tied to it. We need to be careful."

Naomi nodded. "We'll gather more intel and figure out a way to dismantle it safely. Rowan, see if you can find any wards or traps. Cassian, keep watch. Lucian, Sera, you're with me. We'll search for clues about their next move."

As the team dispersed, Naomi caught a glimpse of Sera's troubled expression. The angel's divine knowledge was both a blessing and a burden, and Naomi couldn't shake the feeling that Sera was holding back something critical.

"Whatever you're not telling me," Naomi said quietly, "we need to know. If we're going to stop them, we need the truth.

Sera's gaze softened, but her lips remained a thin line. "Some truths carry a price, Naomi. One, I'm not sure you're ready to pay."

Before Naomi could press further, a distant, echoing chant filled the air. The obelisk began to hum with dark energy, the serpent sigil glowing with an eerie red light.

"They're here," Rowan whispered, her voice barely audible.

Naomi drew her sword, its silver blade gleaming in the moonlight. "Form up! Whatever comes through that portal, we face it together."

As the ground trembled beneath their feet, the team prepared for battle, the shadow of the serpent looming large over Crimson Hollow.

The portal swirled violently, the edges of its molten glyphs cracking and spewing arcs of fiery energy into the air. Its center was a churning vortex of darkness, shot through with streaks of crimson light that pulsed like a heartbeat. The chanting grew louder, as though unseen voices were echoing from within the portal itself, their words ancient and guttural, resonating with unholy power.

From the vortex, shadowy limbs clawed their way into the world, followed by distorted, half–formed faces that screeched in anguish and rage. The portal was no mere gateway; it was a wound in reality, bleeding malevolent energy into the clearing. The ground around the obelisk cracked and smoldered, dark tendrils of magic spreading outward like a living thing, searching for more to corrupt.

Rowan staggered back, her hands in defense. "The portal is tethered to the obelisk! The sigil – it's feeding it power. If we don't sever the connection, it'll fully open, and whatever's on the other side will cross over!"

Lucian cursed under his breath, his crimson eyes narrowing as he assessed the chaos. "If it fully opens, it won't just bring monsters – it'll tear this whole area apart. We need to stop this now."

Naomi gritted her teeth, her sword gleaming as she stepped closer to Sera. "Rowan, can you disrupt the sigil?"

"I can try, but I'll need time!" Rowan shouted over the rising noise.

"You've got it," Naomi said, turning to Lucian and Cassian. "Buy her the time she needs! Keep those things from getting to her!"

As the shadowy forms continued to claw their way through the portal, the team moved into action, the fragile balance of the world hanging by a thread. The portal pulsed again, and this time, the serpent sigil on the obelisk flared bright red, the flames around it roaring higher, as though the cult's ritual had reached its crescendo.

Naomi's voice cut through the chaos. "Rowan, focus on the sigil! Everyone else, hold the line!"

Rowan dropped to her knees in front of the obelisk, her hands trembling as she traced runes in the air. The magical symbols shimmered with a faint green light, forming a protective barrier around her as she began to chant. The air around the obelisk shimmered with resistance, the sigil pulsing violently in response to her spell.

"It's fighting back!" Rowan shouted, sweat beading on her brow as she poured more energy into the incantation. "I can disrupt it, but I need more power!"

Sera stepped forward, her wings glowing brighter as she knelt beside Rowan. Placing a hand on her shoulder, she whispered a divine hymn. Golden light flowed from Sera's touch, intertwining with Rowan's green magic, bolstering the spell.

Lucian and Cassian fought furiously at the edge of the clearing, holding back the shadowy creatures clawing their way through the portal. Lucian's fangs glinted as he tore through a wraith–like figure, while Cassian's claws slashed through another, their teamwork relentless.

Naomi moved to guard Rowan and Sera, her sword a blur of silver as she deflected an oncoming tendril of dark energy. "Hurry up, Rowan! We can't keep this up forever!"

Rowan's voice rose, her chanting becoming a crescendo as the combined magic surged toward the obelisk. The runes on its surface flared, then cracked, the sigil flickering erratically.

"Just a little more!" Rowan screamed, her hands glowing with raw power.

With a final, desperate shout, Rowan slammed her palms onto the ground, and a shockwave of magic erupted outward. The sigil shattered, sending fragments of glowing red energy spiraling into the night. The portal flickered, its edges collapsing inward as it struggled to remain open. The shadowy creatures still inside screeched in rage as the vortex closed with a deafening roar, leaving only silence and scorched earth behind.

Rowan slumped forward, barely caught by Sera before she hit the ground. "It's… It's closed. For now."

Naomi helped her up, her expression grim. "Good work, but this isn't over. That was just a taste of what they're planning."

Sera nodded, her golden blade still glowing in her hand. "They were testing us. They'll try again. And next time, we may not be so lucky."

The team stood amidst the ruins of the clearing, the faint glow of their magic the only light in the encroaching darkness. Tavik Ryn was nowhere to be found. For now, the portal was closed, but the threat of the Ascendants loomed larger than ever.

Chapter 7

Ambush Of the Rogue Pack

The air was thick with the pungent tang of scorched earth and lingering magic as Naomi surveyed the portal site. The scar in reality had closed moments before, the eerie hum of its energy dissipating into the deep, uneasy silence. Around her, the team was gathering their bearings.

Lucian, ever composed, adjusted his dark leather coat, his crimson eyes scanning the charred landscape with predatory precision. "The energy here still feels off," he remarked, voice smooth but edged with caution.

Rowan knelt in the ash-streaked grass, her fingers brushing over the faint glyphs burned into the earth. Her fiery hair gleamed in the moonlight, her face drawn in concentration. "The portal may be gone, but whatever opened it... they left their fingerprints."

Sera, her silver wings tucked against her back, hovered nearby, her silver armor glinting softly. She stood as a living embodiment of purity amid the chaos, her celestial presence both comforting and unnerving. "We should move. This place is... wrong now." Her tone carried an angelic resonance that demanded attention.

Cassian, pacing a short distance away, radiated unease. His wiry frame was tense, his wolf-like eyes darting from shadow to shadow. Even in his human form, the primal energy of the werewolf simmered beneath his skin. "I don't like this," he growled. "Too quiet."

Naomi holstered her pistol and checked her blade. "Stay sharp. Whatever was here might have left a welcoming party."

The words had barely left her lips when the first growl cut through the air – a low, mournful sound that sent a shiver through the team. Cassian froze, his nostrils flaring. "Rogues," he hissed.

From the tree line, shapes emerged: hulking forms with glowing yellow eyes and fur matted with blood. The rogue pack was larger than any Cassian had seen in years. At their center, a figure stood taller than the rest, his form rippling with unnatural strength. Scars crisscrossed his chest, and his snarl revealed teeth far too sharp for a typical werewolf. The Ascendants' mark glowed faintly on his chest, pulsing with malevolent energy.

Naomi drew her blade, its edge catching the moonlight. "Positions! Now!"

The pack charged. Chaos erupted.

Sera launched into the air, her wings a blur as she unleashed radiant blasts of divine energy. Each strike burned through the rogues, sending howls of pain into the night. Rowan's voice rang out in sharp, commanding tones as she wove spells, roots bursting from the ground to ensnare the attackers.

Lucian moved like a liquid shadow, his speed almost too fast to follow. His blade gleamed as he slashed through the rogues with a precision that bordered on artistry. Each strike was deliberate, efficient, and devastating. For the first time, the team noticed the discipline behind his vampiric instincts – there was no frenzy, only his claws extended. His breathing grew ragged.

Cassian, however, was struggling. As the rogues closed in, the scent of blood and the sound of snarls began to overwhelm him. His body tensed, muscles rippling as his claws extended. His breathing grew ragged.

"Cassian!" Naomi barked. "Stay with us!"

But her voice was a distant echo against the storm in his mind. His vision blurred, the line between ally and enemy fading as his wolf surged forward. A rogue leaped at him, and he tore it apart with savage strength – but as he turned, his glowing eyes locked on Sera.

She hesitated, her hands raised in a defensive stance. "Cassian, focus!" she shouted, her voice ringing with divine authority.

Before he could lunge, another rogue slammed into him, knocking him back. The impact seemed to snap him out of his frenzy, and he roared, his fury redirected. With terrifying strength, he tore through the rogues, his movements wild but effective.

Meanwhile, Naomi fought her way to Lucian, cutting down a pair of attackers with swift precision. "You holding up?" she asked, her breath labored.

Lucian smirked, a fang flashing. "I could do this all night. You?"

"Let's not find out," she replied, nodding toward Cassian. We need to get him under control before he turns on us."

Lucian's eyes flickered to the werewolf, who was tearing through the rogues with reckless abandon. "I'll handle him. Cover me."

Naomi hesitated but nodded, trusting the vampire in a way that surprised even herself.

Lucian moved toward Cassian, his voice calm but commanding. "Cassian! Pull yourself together, or I'll put you down myself."

The werewolf spun, growling, his blood-soaked claws flexing. For a moment, it seemed Lucian's words had no effect. Then, something in his tone—or perhaps the unwavering confidence in his stance—cut through the fog of Cassian's rage.

Cassian growled, his chest heaving, but his glowing eyes began to dim. "I'm… fine," he snarled, his voice rough but coherent.

Lucian nodded once. "Good. Now finish the job without getting us killed."

The two turned back to the fray, the unlikely partnership driving the rouges back.

With a final burst of magic from Rowan and a searing blast of light from Sera, the last of the pack fell. Silence returned, broken only by the team's ragged breathing.

Naomi wiped her blade on her coat, surveying the scene. "Everyone in one piece?"

Sera landed lightly beside her, folding her wings. "Barely."

Lucian sheathed his blade, his gaze flickering to Cassian. "You did well. Eventually."

Cassian glared but didn't respond, his shoulders slumping as he fought to regain control.

Rowan stepped forward, her voice soft. "The Ascendants are getting bolder. This was a warning."

Naomi nodded, her jaw tightening. "And we'll answer it. Together."

The team gathered in the aftermath of the battle, their breaths still heavy from the exertion. The moon hung high above them, its light casting long, jagged shadows across the battlefield. Blood and ash mingled with the damp earth, the remnants of the rogue pack littering the ground. A grim silence settled over the group, broken only by the distant rustling of leaves in the wind.

"We need to figure out what the hell that was all about," Naomi said, her voice low but firm. Her dark eyes scanned the field, her mind already working through possibilities.

Lucian crouched beside one of the rogues, examining the faint, glowing mark of the Ascendants etched into its chest. "They weren't here by chance," he said, his fingers tracing the sigil. "This was deliberate. Coordinated."

Sera, standing a few feet away, suddenly stiffened. Her silver wings shifted slightly as her sharp gaze landed on one of the rogues lying among the others. "This one isn't dead," she said, her tone tinged with urgency. She moved swiftly, kneeling beside the werewolf whose shallow breaths barely stirred the air.

The team gathered around her, their weapons still drawn, though more cautiously now. Rowan's hands glowed faintly with emerald magic, ready to act if necessary. Cassian hung back, his jaw tight and his muscles coiled with residual tension.

Naomi nodded at Sera. "See if you can wake him. We need answers."

Sera's hands glowed with a soft, celestial light as she touched the rogue's chest. The werewolf stirred, groaning weakly, his yellow eyes flickering open. They were clouded with pain but still held a glimmer of defiance.

Naomi crouched beside him, her expression hard. "You're going to tell us everything. Who sent you? Was it Tavik Ryn? Where is he? What do the Ascendants want with this portal?"

The rogue coughed, blood staining his lips. His voice was gravelly, broken by the strain of his injuries. "You... don't know... what's coming," he rasped, a bitter smile pulling at his cracked lips.

Rowan leaned in, her voice laced with urgency. "Then tell us. Help us stop it."

The rogue laughed weakly, the sound more like a wheeze. "You can't... stop it. The Ascendants... they're just the beginning."

Cassian growled low in his throat, his patience thinning. "Stop playing games. What's their plan? Why the portals?"

The rogue's gaze shifted to him, his lips curling into a faint snarl. "You'll see soon enough. The balance… will break. They'll tear it apart."

Naomi's eyes narrowed. "The balance between what? Realms? Magic?"

The rogue's breathing grew more labored, his voice barely above a whisper. "All… of it. They want… chaos. A new… order."

Sera's hand pressed more firmly against his chest, her glowing light intensifying as she tried to keep him conscious. "Stay with us. What's their endgame? What are they trying to bring through the portals?"

The rogue's lips moved, but no sound came. His body convulsed, and the glow of the Ascendants' mark on his chest flared briefly before fading. His head slumped back, lifeless.

Sera cursed under her breath, her usually calm demeanor cracking. "He's gone."

Naomi stood, her jaw tight, frustration etched into every line of her face. "Damn it. We were so close."

Lucian rose gracefully, brushing dirt from his hands. "He was barely hanging on. It's a wonder he said as much as he did."

Rowan shook her head, her expression troubled. "They're after more than power. They want to unravel everything. If they break the balance… I don't even know what that would look like."

Cassian, still standing apart from the group, let out a bitter laugh. "It looks like war. Chaos. Exactly what they said. And if they're willing to throw rogue packs at us to make their point, they're not bluffing."

Naomi looked at the group, her voice firm. "This isn't just about stopping the Ascendants anymore. It's about protecting everything – our world, magic, the realms. Whatever they're planning, we're going to need to be ready."

Sera stood, her silver eyes blazing with resolve. We'll need more information. Allies. Resources. If they want to break the balance, we'll have to hold it together."

Lucian's smirk was sharp, his fangs barely visible. "For once, I agree. But if tonight taught us anything, it's that we need to learn to trust each other – or we'll be as dead as him."

The team fell into a heavy silence, the weight of the rogue's cryptic words settling over them. Naomi glanced back at the portal's remnants, a grim determination in her eyes.

"Let's move. We've got work to do."

For the first time, the team stood as something resembling a unit, battle-worn but united in purpose. The night had tested them, and they had survived. As they left the battlefield behind, the night seemed darker than before, the rogue's warning echoing in their minds: You can't stop it. The balance will break.

Chapter 8

Echoes Of the Coven

The command center hummed with tense energy, its dim lighting casting long shadows on the faces of Naomi and her team. The holographic map of the city flickered, dotted with red markers that indicated recent cult activity. Naomi stood at the head of the table, her sharp gaze sweeping over her team.

"This can't be happening," she said, her voice steady but laced with frustration. "Every day, more disappearances. We're missing something, and if we don't figure it out soon, the Ascendants will pull something we can't undo. They're always a step ahead. They've left a trail of bodies, cryptic symbols, and just enough misdirection to keep us chasing shadows. If we don't change our approach, we're going to lose whatever edge we have left."

"Agreed," Cassian said, his gravelly voice cutting through the tension. "But every lead we've followed has been a dead end. Literally."

Sera, her silver wings faintly glowing, leaned forward, resting her elbows on the table. "The cult's rituals are escalating. Their power is growing. Whatever they're planning, they're close. We need to cut them off before they reach full strength."

Lucian lounged against the far wall, his dark attire blending into the shadows. His crimson eyes gleamed. "We know they're after something ancient. Something dangerous. The question is, how do we find them before they use it?"

Rowan crossed her arms, her emerald eyes troubled. "They're using old magic. I can feel it. There might be a way," she said hesitantly. "But it's risky. If we want to track them, we'll need to fight fire with fire." Cassian turned to her, his broad frame tense with barely contained energy. "What kind of risky?"

Rowan hesitated, the weight of her words pressing down on her. "An ancient locator spell. It's powerful and dangerous… but it might give us the answers we need. I'd need my grimoire to cast it – and I'd need Lucian to come with me. My shop's wards won't let anyone else inside."

Lucian stepped forward. "I'll go with her."

"You sure?" Naomi asked, her piercing gaze shifting to the Vampire. "The last time we split up–"

"I'll keep her safe," Lucian interrupted, his tone leaving no room for argument.

Naomi nodded. "Do it. But keep us updated. Sera, Cassian, and I will work here to prepare for anything you find. Stay safe."

Lucian straightened, a sly smirk playing on his lips. "Ready when you are, witch."

Rowan rolled her eyes, but a faint smile tugged at her lips. "Let's go."

The air outside Rowan's shop was thick with the scent of herbs and faint traces of ozone, a byproduct of the witch's wards.

Lucian followed her inside, his footsteps eerily silent against the creaking wooden floor. The shop was dimly lit, a chaotic yet enchanting mix of books, jars, and artifacts, each shelf telling its own story and giving it an otherworldly feel. Rowan moved with purpose, navigating the clutter to a locked cabinet beneath the counter. She pulled an ancient, leather-bound book from a hidden compartment. The grimoire was old, its edges worn and its cover etched with runes that glowed faintly under her touch.

"This is it," she said. She set it on the counter, her fingers trailing over the worn cover.

"Are you sure about this?" Lucian asked, his crimson eyes narrowing. "You said it's dangerous, so what's the catch?"

Rowan sighed, opening the book and flipping through the yellowed pages to a page filled with intricate symbols. "The spell requires a blood offering. Mine. It'll link me to whatever we're tracking. The dangerous part... If the connection is too strong, it could–"

"Burn you out," Lucian finished, his tone uncharacteristically serious. "You don't have to do this alone."

"I know. But this spell... It's personal. If the Ascendants aren't stopped, more people will die. Besides, if we don't take risks, we'll never stop them, and I'm not letting that happen."

She cleared a space on the floor, drawing a complex sigil with chalk. Candles flickered to life around her as she began chanting in a language that made the air vibrate with unseen power and thicken with magic. Lucian watched, tension coiling in his chest.

He'd seen magic before, but this was different–raw and unbridled.

The symbols on the page glowed, and a faint golden thread appeared, snaking through the air. Rowan winced as she pricked her finger, letting a drop of blood fall onto the page. The thread brightened, pulling taut as it pointed toward a direction. As Rowan's voice grew louder, the room darkened, shadows pooling in the corners. The sigil flared with blinding light, and Rowan let out a gasp, collapsing to her knees.

"Rowan?" Lucian was at her side in an instant, catching her before she fell. "You're pushing yourself too hard."

"I'm fine," she murmured, though her face was pale and her voice wavered. "The spell worked."

"What did you see?" he asked, his voice low.

"It's leading us to the old cathedral on the outskirts of the city," she whispered. "Abandoned. And… faces. People, I thought I left behind." She shuddered. "My old coven. They're connected to this. Somehow."

Lucian frowned. "Your coven? I thought you said–"

"Long story," she cut him off, her tone sharp. "Let's just say I didn't leave on good terms."

Lucian didn't press her, but he could see the shadows of her past in her eyes. "We need to call Naomi. If this cathedral is where the cult is hiding, we'll need the whole team."

Rowan nodded as Lucian pulled out his phone, texting Naomi the location. "Let's move before you collapse."

As they traveled, Rowan's thoughts drifted to her coven. Her memories came in flashes–heated arguments, accusations of recklessness, and their ultimate decision to banish her. Their strict adherence to tradition had clashed with Rowan's innovative approach to magic, and her refusal to back down had cost her everything.

But now, she couldn't shake the feeling that her coven was somehow tied to the Ascendants. Their obsession with purity and power mirrored the cult's ideology too closely to be a coincidence.

The derelict cathedral loomed before them, its crumbling walls and shattered stained glass casting eerie reflections in the moonlight. Rowan shivered as they stepped inside, the golden thread trying to pull her deeper into the darkened space.

Naomi, Sera, and Cassian arrived moments later. "What are we looking at?" Naomi asked.

Rowan pointed to the altar, where strange symbols were carved into the stone. A Pile of bloodstained robes lay nearby, and a faint glow emanated from the crypt below.

Cassian sniffed the air, his expression darkened. "This place reeks of death. More victims. Recently killed," Cassian muttered, his sharp senses on high alert.

Sera's wings flared as she moved closer to the altar, her expression grim. "There's something written here. It's a prophecy."

Naomi stepped beside her, reading aloud: "When the blood of the chosen stains the earth, the ascension shall begin."

Lucian's voice was cold. "They're not just sacrificing people. They're preparing for something big."

Rowan swayed, clutching her head as the golden thread dissolved into smoke. "They know we're here," she whispered. "And they're ready for us."

Naomi's hand rested on her holstered sidearm. "Stay sharp. We don't know what we're walking into."

A low rumble echoed through the cathedral, and the team drew their weapon, bracing for whatever came next. The group moved cautiously through the cathedral's shattered doors, the interior lit by the sinister glow of moonlight filtering through stained glass. The air was thick with the scent of decay, and the faint sound of chanting echoed from below.

Rowan froze, her eyes widening. "The crypt. They're down there."

They descended into the darkness, the air growing colder with each step. At the bottom, they found a chamber filled with strange carvings and more victims–bodies arranged in a twisted mockery of worship. In the center of the room was another larger altar, its surface etched with runes similar to those seen on the altar outside.

Naomi stepped forward, her voice steady despite the horror surrounding them. "What does it mean?"

Rowan examined the carvings, her fingers tracing the lines. "It's a prophecy. Something about the ascension… and a sacrifice." Her voice faltered. "They're trying to summon something. Something powerful."

Lucian's jaw tightened. "Then we stop them. Whatever it takes."

Chapter 9

Crypt Of Corruption

The crypt was deathly silent now, its cool, stale air laced with a faint metallic tang of blood and sulfur. Whoever was down here was gone now. Naomi led the way, her black military coat fluttering behind her as she stepped cautiously into the next chamber. Sera followed closely, her glow casting a faint light on the ancient stone walls. Lucian moved with predatory grace, his crimson eyes scanning the darkness, while Cassian growled low, his heightened senses on edge. Rowan trailed, her fingers twitching with latent magical energy, ready to act at the first sign of danger.

The chamber at the heart of the crypt was massive, its vaulted ceiling held aloft by ornate pillars carved with runes that pulsed faintly with residual magic. At its center lay a summoning circle, its intricate design scorched into the stone floor. The runes glimmered faintly with malevolent energy, and in the center of the circle lay charred remains, evidence of a ritual gone awry.

"This is where they tried to bring it through," Rowan murmured, her voice trembling with a mixture of awe and disgust. She knelt beside the circle, tracing one of the runes with a gloved hand. "These markings… they're not just summoning sigils. They're a binding, meant to tether whatever they called to this plane."

Sera's wings shifted uneasily. "The energy is still potent. They were summoning something far beyond their control. But the ritual was interrupted. Likely by their own incompetence–or by design."

Lucian crouched near a discarded tome, its leather cover marked with the emblem of the Ascendants, the secretive cult they had been tracking for days.

He opened it carefully, his fangs glinting in the faint light as he scanned the pages. "These notes mention a benefactor– someone funding their work. It doesn't name them outright, but…" He flipped a page and hissed softly. These codes are familiar. They're used in Eterna's upper echelons."

Naomi stiffened, her hand instinctively going to the hilt of her sword. "You're saying someone in the government is involved?"

Lucian rose smoothly to his feet. "Not just involved. Complicit. This level of funding and protection doesn't come from small players. They had access to resources only the elite could provide."

Cassian growled, his claws extending slightly. "So, while we've been risking our necks hunting these fanatics, someone powerful has been pulling the strings."

The revelation weighed on the team as they continued to search the chamber. Naomi's sharp eyes caught sight of a small, sealed envelope tucked into the corner of the ancient altar. Breaking the seal, she unfolded the parchment, her expression darkening with each word she read.

It's worse than we thought," Naomi said grimly. "This document links high-ranking officials directly to the Ascendants. They've been orchestrating this from the shadows, likely for years. And this–" She held up the envelope, which bore the official seal of the Council of Eterna. "This proves they're tied to the city's leadership."

The team exchanged uneasy glances, the gravity of the situation sinking in. Sera's voice broke the silence. "We cannot ignore this. If the government itself is tainted, the corruption runs deeper than we imagined."

Before Naomi could respond, her communicator crackled to life. A cold, authoritative voice came through, unmistakably one of her superiors. "Captain Blackwood, we have received word of your investigation. Cease all activity immediately and return to headquarters. This matter is classified."

Naomi's jaw clenched as she shut off the device without responding. She turned to the team, her eyes burning with defiance. "They're trying to silence us."

"They're scared," Cassian growled. "We've uncovered too much."

"But if we go up against them," Rowan said, her voice tinged with fear, "We'll be painting targets on our backs. The Council won't hesitate to eliminate us to protect their secrets."

Lucian crossed his arms, his expression unreadable. "So, what's the plan, Captain? Justice or self-preservation?"

Naomi's eyes darted between her team, weighing their expressions. They were loyal, but this would be a dangerous road. Sera stepped forward, her serene voice steady. "If we let this go, the cycle of corruption will continue. Innocent lives will be lost."

Cassian snarled, his claws raking against the stone wall. "I'm not one to run from a fight. If we're going to take them down, we need to hit them where it hurts."

Rowan hesitated, but the determination in her companions' eyes gave her courage. "I've seen enough of the Council's hypocrisy to know they need to be stopped. I'm in."

Lucian smirked, his fangs glinting. "A noble cause with a high probability of death? Count me in."

Naomi felt a swell of pride at their resolve. She squared her shoulders, her voice firm. "Then it's settled. We expose the truth, no matter the cost."

As they left the crypt, the weight of the decision pressed on them, but so did the clarity of purpose. The fight ahead would be brutal, but for the first time, they were united in a cause that transcended their differences. Naomi gave the team orders to head back to Command and start digging into every lead they could while she headed to HQ.

Naomi strode through the polished marble halls of Eterna's Central Command, her boots echoing sharply with each step.

The grandeur of the building—an architectural marvel of stone and steel—felt suffocating, its imposing pillars and vaulted ceilings a stark reminder of the power wielded within these walls. Naomi adjusted her black coat, the insignia of her rank gleaming on her shoulder, as she approached the heavy oak doors of the Council chamber.

Two armored sentries flanked the entrance, their faces hidden behind emotionless helmets. They stepped aside in unison as she approached, one of them opening the door. Inside, the atmosphere was tense, a silence heavy with unspoken judgment.

The chamber was circular, with a raised dais at the center where five members of the Council sat behind a crescent-shaped table. Each cloaked in dark robes, their faces partially obscured by shadow. Behind them, the massive emblem of the city–a golden phoenix rising from a crown–gleamed in the soft glow of enchanted lights.

Naomi stood in the center of the room, her back straight, her hand resting lightly on the hilt of her sword. She made no effort to hide her disdain for the charade of authority these individuals represented.

"Captain Blackwood," intoned the central figure, Councilor Draeven, a man known for his icy demeanor and ruthless efficiency. His fiery red hair and sharp features gave him an air of gravitas, but his pale blue eyes betrayed no warmth. "You've been summoned to clarify the activities of your task force. Specifically, your unauthorized investigation into the crypt beneath the Old Quarter."

Naomi inclined her head slightly, her expression carefully neutral. "With respect, Councilor, the investigation was authorized under Directive 47-C, which grants my task force discretionary power to pursue threats to the city."

"Do not lecture us on the law," snapped Councilor Brionne, a woman whose voice was as sharp as the emerald brooch she wore. "The investigation into the crypt was not within your purview. The Ascendants were deemed a low-priority threat months ago."

Naomi's jaw tightened, but she kept her tone measured. "With all due respect, Councilor, the evidence we uncovered proves otherwise. The Ascendants' activities in the crypt indicate they were attempting to summon an entity of immense power. Had they succeeded, the consequences would have been catastrophic."

"And yet they failed," Brionne replied coldly. "A hypothetical threat is no justification for exceeding your authority."

"Hypothetical?" Naomi's composure cracked, her voice rising. "We found direct evidence linking high-ranking officials to the cult. This isn't just about the Ascendants—it's about corruption at the highest levels of our government."

Her words hung in the air like a thunderclap. The Council exchanged uneasy glances, their calm facade momentarily disrupted. Draeven leaned forward, his eyes narrowing.

"Captain," he said slowly, "you are treading dangerous ground. Accusations of this magnitude require irrefutable proof, and yet you stand here with little more than conjecture."

Naomi stepped closer to the dais, her defiance unyielding. "The documents we recovered are more than conjecture. They contain coded communications, financial records, and personal correspondence implicating key figures in this very Council."

The room fell deathly silent. Councilor Brionne's face darkened, while Councilor Vorlan, a burly man with a thick beard, shifted uncomfortably in his seat.

"You will hand over all evidence immediately," Draeven said, his tone leaving no room for argument. "This investigation is hereby terminated. Your task force will disband, effective immediately."

Naomi stared at him, her heart pounding. "You can't be serious. The people deserve to know the truth. If we stop now, the corruption festering in this city will continue to grow."

Draeven's expression hardened. "Your loyalty is to Eterna, Captain, not to your personal sense of justice. The stability of this city depends on discretion. Pursuing this line of inquiry will only spread chaos."

"Chaos?" Naomi's voice was sharp now. "The chaos is already here, hiding behind gilded walls and false promises. You're asking me to betray everything I stand for."

Brionne leaned forward, her emerald brooch catching the light. "We are ordering you, Captain. If you defy this Council, you will face severe consequences. Your rank, your career, your life–they all hang in the balance."

Naomi's fingers tightened around the hilt of her sword, her mind racing. She had known this confrontation would come, but the naked display of corruption still churned her stomach. For a moment, she considered compliance–pretending to obey while working in secret. But the faces of her team flashed in her mind: Sera's quiet conviction, Lucian's ruthless cunning, Cassian's unshakable loyalty, Rowan's fierce determination. They had chosen justice, and so would she.

Straightening her spine, Naomi met Draeven's gaze head-on. "Do what you must, Councilor. But I will not stop. Not until the truth is revealed."

The room erupted into angry murmurs, but Naomi turned on her heel and strode out before anyone could stop her. The weight of her decision bore down on her shoulders, but she felt a fierce clarity. Her path was set, and there was no turning back.

As the heavy doors closed behind her, the late afternoon sun dipped below the horizon, casting Eterna in a cloak of twilight as Naomi exited Central Command.

The weight of her defiance in the Council chamber pressed heavily on her shoulders, yet she kept her stride purposeful, her hand resting instinctively on the pommel of her sword. She felt a faint ripple of magic in the air. Rowan's voice whispered through the small enchanted charm Naomi carried in her pocket. "How did it go?"

Naomi allowed herself a small, grim smile. "We're officially rogue."

Rowan's soft chuckle echoed in reply. "Good. Then we're right where we need to be."

Naomi thought for a moment. "I need the team to get to the safehouse now. I'm on my way there."

As she approached the task force's command center, her communicator emitted a sharp chime. Frowning, Naomi retrieved it from her inside coat pocket. The encrypted screen displayed a name that made her pause: Councilor Vorlan.

"Blackwood," she answered cautiously.

The voice on the other end was gruff, hushed. "Captain, I need to speak to you. Privately."

"After that display in the chamber, I'm not inclined to trust anyone on the Council." Naomi's tone was biting.

"I don't blame you," Vorlan admitted, his voice tinged with weariness. "But I'm not calling as your enemy. If you're willing to listen, meet me at the old Ember Station near the industrial quarter in an hour. Come alone."

Naomi hesitated. This could easily be a trap—a way for the Council to neutralize her after her defiance. But Vorlan had looked uneasy during the meeting, his shifting demeanor contrasting with the cold resolve of the other members. If there was even a chance he could provide valuable information, it was worth the risk.

"Fine," she said at last. "But if this is a setup, you'll regret it."

"Noted," Vorlan replied before disconnecting.

Naomi turned around and headed to the Forge, reaching in her pocket and touching the charm again. She needed to communicate with Rowan and the team about her destination, just in case this was a setup.

The Ember Station was a relic of Eterna's past, its massive stone structure long abandoned as the city's industrial advancements rendered it obsolete. Now, its soot-stained walls and looming smokestacks stood as a forgotten monument in the shadow of towering skyscrapers.

Naomi slipped into the forge's cavernous interior, her steps silent against the cracked stone floor. The faint scent of rust and oil lingered in the air, mingling with the faint hum of distant traffic.

A dim lantern's light glowed near the center of the space, where Vorlan stood waiting, his thick frame silhouetted against the gloom. He wore no Council robes, only a simple overcoat that made him seem less imposing and more human.

"You actually came," Vorlan said, his deep voice carrying a note of approval.

"I've faced worse than a disillusioned Councilor," Naomi replied coolly, keeping her distance. "Why are we here, Vorlan? I don't have time for games." He turned to face her fully, his expression grim. "I don't have time for games either. I reached out because I believe you're right about the Council, about corruption. And I'm tired of turning a blind eye."

Naomi studied him, searching for any sign of deceit. "You didn't speak up in the chamber. You sat there and let them bury the truth."

Vorlan sighed heavily, running a hand through his beard. "And what good would it have done? You saw how they shut you down. Brionne, Draeven–they've been consolidating power for years. I don't have the influence to challenge them outright, but I've seen enough to know they're hiding something bigger."

"Then tell me what you know," Naomi demanded, stepping closer.

Vorlan hesitated, his gaze darting to the shadows as if fearing they had ears. "For months, I've been hearing whispers–projects being funded off the books, entire divisions in Central Command answering only to select Council members. They claim it's to protect Eterna, but their secrecy suggests otherwise. Then there's the Ascendants... I wouldn't be surprised if Draeven and Brionne were funneling resources to them."

Naomi folded her arms. "Why would the Council back a cult?"

"That's what I've been trying to figure out," Vorlan said, lowering his voice. "There's a project they've referred to as The Herald's Descent. I don't know the details, but it involves ancient magic and significant resources. The Ascendants were just a pawn–a means to an end."

Naomi's stomach churned at the mention of the name. "The Herald's Descent? Sounds like a doomsday plan."

Vorlan nodded grimly. "Whatever it is, it's dangerous. And they're willing to kill to keep it a secret. You've made yourself a target, Captain. They'll come for you and your team."

Naomi narrowed her eyes. "And why should I believe you're not part of this conspiracy?"

"Because if I were, you'd already be dead," Volan said bluntly. "I'm risking my life by even speaking to you. If they find out I've been digging into this, I'll be silenced like everyone else who's gotten too close."

Naomi's hand twitched near her sword, but she kept her posture steady. "If you're telling the truth, then you need to help me expose them. Provide evidence. Names."

Vorlan shook his head. "Evidence is hard to come by. Draeven and Brionne cover their tracks too well. But there's a vault beneath Central Command—hidden records, correspondence, everything they're trying to bury. If you can access it, you'll have the proof you need."

"And how do you suggest I break into the most secure location in Eterna?" Naomi asked dryly.

Vorlan smirked faintly. "You're resourceful. If anyone can pull it off, it's you. But I can provide codes to bypass the outer security layers and a map of the facility. After that, you're on your own."

Naomi studied him for a long moment. "Why are you doing this, Vorlan?"

His smirk faded, replaced by a look of weariness. "Because I swore an oath to serve Eterna, not the ambitions of corrupt bureaucrats. And because I want to believe this city can still be saved."

Naomi nodded, pocketing the codes and map he handed her. "If this is a trap, I'll make sure you regret it."

Vorlan chuckled darkly. "If this is a trap, Captain, I won't live long enough to regret anything."

With that, he extinguished the lantern and disappeared into the shadows, leaving Naomi to contemplate the dangerous road ahead. For the first time, she felt a flicker of hope—but also the crushing weight of the task before her. Justice would be their weapon, and they would wield it against the shadows that threatened to consume Eterna.

Chapter 10

Fractures in the Ranks

Naomi's boots pounded against the cobblestones as she made her way to the team's safehouse near Central Command. Her mind was a storm of thoughts–Vorlan's warnings, the looming threat of The Herald's Descent, and the delicate tightrope her team was walking between justice and survival. She gripped the hilt of her sword tightly, bracing herself for whatever awaited her.

As she approached the old warehouse, a fortress of brick, steel, and reinforced glass, muffled voices reached her ears, sharp and angry. Her brow furrowed, and she slipped in through the side door, her senses on high alert.

The air inside was thick with tension, suffocating in its intensity. The makeshift war room, dimly lit by flickering monitors, felt more like a cage than a sanctuary.

She maneuvered to the center of the room, her hands gripping the edge of the command console. The holographic map of the enemy's stronghold glowed cold and blue, but no one was paying attention to the tactical display. The team had recently been through a battle together, but the cracks in their unity were becoming impossible to ignore.

"Stop posturing, you overgrown mutt," Lucian sneered at Cassian, his eyes flashing with disdain. They were locked in a heated argument, their voices rising with every exchange. Lucian leaned against the far wall, his arms crossed, but the sharpness of his tone betrayed his frustration. His eyes narrowed as he watched Cassian. "If you'd stop letting your temper dictate your actions, we might actually make some progress."

Cassian's claws extended, scraping audibly against the floor. His eyes burned with fury. "You're one to talk, leech. Always slinking around, whispering in the shadows. What aren't you telling us?"

Lucian's smirk widened, but the amusement didn't reach his eyes. "Not everything is about you, wolf. Maybe you should focus on doing your job instead of looking for someone to blame."

"That's rich, coming from the guy who thinks he's too good to fight on the front lines," Cassian snapped, taking a menacing step forward.

"That's enough!" Naomi's voice cracked through the air like a whip, but neither man paid her any attention.

Rowan, standing by the edge of the room with her arms crossed, rolled her eyes. "Let them fight," she muttered. "Maybe they'll knock some sense into each other."

Sera stood apart from the others. Her serene exterior belied the storm brewing within her as she stared at the glowing map on the central console. She had been silent until now. She stepped forward, her glowing silver eyes flicking between Lucian and Cassian. "You're both acting like children," she said, her voice calm but carrying an undercurrent of divine authority.

"This fighting helps no one."

Cassian turned on her, his anger redirected. "And you're no better, angel," he growled. "Always floating above us, keeping your secrets. How are we supposed to trust you when you won't even tell us what you know?"

Rowan seized the moment, her voice sharp and accusatory. "He's right. You've been holding back, Sera. What are you hiding? What aren't you telling us about the enemy?"

Sera's serene composure faltered for the briefest moment, and that was enough. Rowan pressed forward, her green eyes blazing. "You claim to be on our side, but how do we know that? You've been vague about everything–where you came from, why you're here, and what the hell you know about the enemy's plans."

Naomi slammed her fist on the console, the holographic map flickering. "Enough!" She barked, her voice cutting through the room like a blade. "All of you, stand down!"

But the damage had been done. The team stood in tense silence, each member glaring at another.

Finally, Naomi exhaled, her shoulders sagging. "This isn't working," she said, her tone weary but firm. "We can't fight a war if we're fighting each other. Take a break. Cool Off. We'll regroup in an hour."

Without another word, the team began to disperse, each retreating to a different corner of the base to lick their wounds.

Cassian stormed out of the command room and into the dense forest that surrounded the base. The cool night air did little to quell the fire raging inside him. Memories of his pack flooded his mind–his brothers and sisters, all slaughtered in a single night. He blamed himself for their deaths, and now he could feel the same failure creeping into his team.

He punched a tree, the bark splintering under his fist. "Damn him," he growled under his breath, thinking of Lucian. "Damn all of them." But even he seethed, a nagging voice in the back of his mind whispered that the real problem wasn't Lucian. It was him.

Lucian retreated to the shadows of the base's lower levels, the cool, damp air comforting in its familiarity. He leaned against the cold stone wall, spinning a silver dagger between his fingers. Cassian's words had hit closer to home than he wanted to admit. He did keep secrets–too many of them. But he had learned long ago that trust was a dangerous thing. He'd lost everything once because of that misplaced trust. He wouldn't make the same mistake again. Still, a part of him wondered if he was wrong.

Rowan paced in the library, her fingers trailing over the spines of ancient books. Her frustration with Sera boiled over into anger. She hated secrets, and she hated feeling like a pawn in someone else's game. Grabbing an old tome, she slammed it onto the table and began flipping through its pages. If Sera wouldn't tell her the truth, she would find it herself.

Sera knelt in the base's chapel, her wings unfurled and glowing faintly in the dim light. She clasped her hands together, her lips moving in silent prayer. She knew she was losing the team's trust, but she couldn't bring herself to reveal everything she knew. The truth was too dangerous, too overwhelming. She had seen what happened when mortals were exposed to the full scope of the celestial war. But she couldn't shake the feeling that withholding the truth was just as dangerous.

Naomi stayed in the command room, staring at the map. The weight of leadership pressed heavily on her shoulders. She had always prided herself on keeping her team together, but this time, she wasn't sure if she could. The team was breaking apart, and the enemy was getting closer. She had to find a way to bring them back together before it was too late. But first, she had to confront her own doubts.

The hour passed in heavy silence, each member of the team wrestling with their emotions and doubts. One by one, they returned to the command room, their steps reluctant but deliberate. Naomi stood at the front of the room, her arms crossed and her gaze set with the determination of a captain unwilling to let her crew fall apart. Sera was the first to return. Her expression was serene but tinged with sadness, her silver eyes meeting Naomi's briefly before she settled into her place by the console. Next came Rowan, her demeanor guarded and her green eyes sharp, as if daring someone to challenge her. Lucian appeared shortly after, moving with his usual grace, though his crimson gaze betrayed an underlying tension. Finally, Cassian entered, his broad shoulders squared, though his claws remained sheathed–a small sign of progress.

Naomi surveyed them, her intense stare moving to each member of her fractured team. The tension was thick, the silence heavy, but she had no intention of letting this spiral further.

"Good," she said, her voice breaking the stillness. You're all here. Now, let's talk."

Lucian smirked faintly, though it lacked his usual bite. "I don't think talking is our strong suit." "Exactly why we're doing it," Naomi said firmly. "This team doesn't work unless we trust each other. Right now, that trust is gone. So, we fix it. Here. Now."

"I'll start," Rowan said, her voice firm but measured. "Sera, I don't trust you. I want to, but you've been holding back. I don't know what you're afraid of, but we're fighting for our lives out here. We deserve the truth."

Sera met Rowan's gaze, her wings shifting slightly as if to shield herself. She took a deep breath, the glow of her silver eyes dimming. "You're right," she admitted softly. "I have been holding back, but not because I don't trust you. It's because I fear what the truth will do to you."

Rowan's brow furrowed, her frustration evident. "You don't get to make that decision for us. We're in this together, or not at all."

Sera hesitated, her hands clasped tightly. "The enemy we face… they're more than just an army or a cult. They're connected to the Celestial Divide–the fracture between Heaven and Hell. If we fail, it's not just this world that will fall. It's all of existence." Her voice was heavy with regret. "I didn't tell you because I didn't want to burden you with the weight of it."

The room fell silent as the weight of her words sank in. Even Lucian, typically quick with a sarcastic quip, said nothing. Finally, it was Cassian who spoke.

"You think we can't handle it?" he growled, though his tone was less accusatory and more resigned. "We're already fighting monsters. What's one more apocalyptic threat?"

Lucian stood near a table, his crimson eyes flaring as he jabbed a finger toward Cassian. "You think brute strength is enough to get us through this? Your recklessness is going to get us killed." Cassian snarled, his claws twitching as he took a step closer.

"At least I don't hide in the shadows, waiting to pick off scraps like some scavenger. Maybe if you took a real risk for once, we wouldn't be in this mess."

No one spoke, their collective silence a testament to their unease. Finally, Rowan stepped forward, breaking the stalemate.

Sera nodded, her expression softening. "You're stronger than I gave you credit for. I see that now. I'm sorry for doubting you."

Rowan exhaled slowly, some of her tension easing. "We don't need you to shield us, Sera. We need you to stand with us."

"I will," Sera promised, her voice steady.

Naomi nodded, satisfied with the exchange. "Good. Now, Lucian and Cassian, do you two want to explain what the fight was about?" Cassian and Lucian exchanged a glance, their mutual animosity still simmering but less volatile. Cassian was the first to speak.

"He thinks he's better than the rest of us," Cassian said bluntly. "Always acting like he's got it all figured out."

Lucian's smirk returned, though it was tempered with a rare hint of vulnerability. "And you think I'm hiding something. You're not wrong." He straightened, his tone losing its usual sarcasm. "I've spent centuries learning to survive by keeping secrets. It's not personal. It's just… how I've stayed alive."

Cassian growled softly, but Naomi cut in before he could respond. "And do you trust this team, Lucian?" Lucian hesitated, his crimson eyes meeting Naomi's. "I'm trying," he admitted. "But trust doesn't come easy for me."

Cassian's shoulders relaxed slightly. "Then stop acting like we're your enemies," he said, his voice gruff but less hostile. "We've got enough of those already."

"Enough!" Rowan's voice cut through, but it was laced with frustration. "Both of you are acting like idiots. While you're busy measuring egos, the Council is probably already covering their tracks. If we're not careful, this whole mission is going to fall apart!"

"And whose fault is that?" Sera's usually calm tone was icy, her wings shifting as her luminous eyes bore into Rowan. "Your wards nearly collapsed during our last fight. If they had, we wouldn't be standing here."

Rowan's hands clenched, green sparks flickering at her fingertips. "Oh, so now it's my fault. Maybe if you stopped playing the untouchable angel and trusted us, we'd work better as a team!"

Naomi's gaze swept over the team. She slammed her fists on the console. All eyes turned toward her as she stepped forward, her voice cold and commanding.

Cassian and Lucian exchanged glares but said nothing. Rowan folded her arms, while Sera turned away, her feathers bristling.

"What the hell is happening here? We're fighting a war on all sides, and this is what I come back to? Petty arguments and finger-pointing? We don't have time for this. The Council is coming for us, and if we're not united, they'll tear us apart. This mission is bigger than any of us," she said, her tone firm but not unkind. "We don't have to be perfect, but we do have to be united. If we can't trust each other, we've already lost. So whatever judges or doubts you're holding, bury them. Now"

The silence hung heavy, the team exchanging uncertain glances. Naomi's voice softened slightly, but her resolve remained firm. "We're in this together, or not at all. Make your choice."

Slowly, the tension eased. Cassian backed down first, muttering something under his breath, while Lucian exhaled and crossed his arms. Rowan's sparks faded, and Sera gave a slight nod, her feathers settling. The team nodded, the weight of her words settling over them. For the first time in hours, the room felt less oppressive. There was still tension, still lingering doubts, but there was also a sense of renewed purpose.

Naomi let out a quiet breath. The cracks in their unity were evident, but for now, the fire had been quelled. She just hoped it would hold long enough for them to survive what was coming.

"All right," Naomi said, stepping back to the console. "Let's get to work. We have a world to save."

Naomi now stood at the center of the dimly lit safehouse, the team gathered around her. The air was still heavy with tension from their earlier argument, but the lantern light cast enough warmth to keep it from boiling over again. Each member watched her with varying expressions.

She took a deep breath, knowing the gravity of what she was about to share. "I met with Councilor Vorlan tonight."

That got their attention. Lucian's eyes narrowed, and Cassian folded his arms. Sera tilted her head slightly, her feathers bristling again, while Rowan frowned.

The team was splintered, their unity shattered by anger, distrust, and secrets. As they each confronted their inner demons, the clock continued to tick. Now the team was gathered around the map, their movements were less tense, their words less sharp. They weren't perfect, but they were trying. And for now, that was enough. They would have to decide: would they stand together, or would they fall apart?

"He reached out," Naomi continued. "Said he believes me—believes us. He knows the Council is hiding something, that Tavik Ryn is involved, and he's tired of turning a blind eye."

"And we're just supposed to trust him? Lucian said, his voice dripping with skepticism. "Sounds convenient that he suddenly grew a conscience."

"I don't trust him," Naomi admitted. "But he gave me something we can use. He mentioned a vault underneath Central Command–records, documents, correspondence, evidence. If we can get in, we might be able to expose everything, or at least gather some important intel. He mentioned names, specifically Tavik's top secret project funding, and whatever this Herald's Descent project is."

Rowan's eyes widened. "The Herald's Descent? That sounds ominous. Did he say what it is?"

Naomi shook her head. "No, but whatever it is, it's tied to Valik and the Ascendants. He believes it is the key to understanding what the Council is really up to."

"Let me guess," Cassian said, his tone edged with sarcasm. "He gave us just enough information to throw ourselves into the fire and left out the part where this is probably a death trap."

"Pretty much," Naomi replied dryly. "But he did give me codes to bypass the outer security and a map of the facility. It's not much, but it's a start."

Sera's voice was calm but firm. "And what happens if he's setting us up? If this vault is a trap, we'll be walking right into their hands."

Naomi met her gaze. "It's a risk, I know. But if he's telling the truth, this could be our best shot at bringing them down. We've been running in circles, chasing shadows. This is something concrete. Something we can use."

Lucian leaned back against the wall, his crimson eyes thoughtful. "Breaking into Central Command isn't just risky—it's suicide. The place is locked down tighter than a fortress, and the moment we're spotted, the entire city will be after us."

Rowan crossed her arms, her expression troubled. "It's not just about breaking in. Even if we succeed, what then? Exposing the truth is one thing, but what happens when the Council turns the public against us? They control the narrative."

Naomi glanced at each of them, her voice steady. "I won't lie to you. This won't be easy. It's dangerous, and it could very well cost us our lives. But if we don't act, the corruption continues unchecked. More lives will be lost. I can't promise we'll succeed, but I promise this: we won't give up without a fight."

Cassian let out a growl, but there was a grudging respect in his tone. "I've made it this far by fighting. Might as well keep going." Sera nodded, her serene expression resolute. "If this is the path to justice, I'll follow it." Rowan sighed but gave a faint smile. "Guess I'll be the one keeping you all alive, then."

Lucian smirked faintly, his fangs flashing. "Well, if we're going to storm a fortress, I'd prefer doing it with all of you. Let's make sure we leave a mark."

"Ok," Naomi said with excitement in her voice. "First, I need each of you to reach out to your confidential informants, old friends, contacts, whoever you can find, and fast. We need a line on Tavik. If we can find him, then maybe we can find out what role he plays in all this."

Chapter 11

Darkness of Redhaven

The flickering neon lights of Redhaven Quarter painted the wet cobblestones in shifting hues of crimson, violet, and gold. The district was alive with its usual buzz of shifting and chaos, a haven for those who thrived on the fringes of supernatural society. It was here, amidst the sinuous alleyways and shadowy corners, that the team began their search for answers.

Naomi's revelation about corruption in the Council and the name Tavik Ryn had left the team with more questions than answers. The Ascendants–a cult shrouded in secrecy–was a dangerous thread to pull on, but it was the only lead they had. And now, Tavik's name was surfacing in whispers, tied to strange activities in Redhaven.

Cassian prowled through the crowded streets with his usual predatory grace. His heightened senses picked up the faint, coppery tang of blood mingling with the scent of damp earth and decay. The werewolf was meeting Zarek, a half-demon informant who owed Cassian more than a few favors. Zarek was known for skimming the underbelly of Redhaven's darkest corners, and if Tavik were stirring up trouble, Zarek would know.

Cassian found him lurking near the entrance of the Oblivion Den, a rundown speakeasy that catered to Redhaven's less savory inhabitants. Zarek's sharp eyes flickered nervously as Cassian approached.

"Tavik Ryn?" Cassian growled, his deep voice barely above a whisper. "What do you know?"

Zarek licked his lips and glanced over his shoulder. "Word is he's been asking about… items. Not the kind you buy at the marketplace, you know? Astrion would never allow that. Dark stuff. Artifacts, rare ingredients. Stuff that screams trouble."

Cassian's eyes narrowed. "Where?"

"Lots of places. But the Abyssal Chalice–you know it? That bar where no one with a clean conscience dares set foot. He's been spotted there a couple of times." While Cassian headed back to the safe house to fill the team in, Rowan was meeting her own contact.

Rowan had taken a different route, slipping into a quieter part of Redhaven where the air hummed with latent magic. She was meeting Corin, a warlock and an old friend from her days studying magic in the Crescent Archives. Corin had a knack for keeping his ear to the ground, especially when it came to magic users dabbling in forbidden arts.

The small, candlelit shop where they met was cluttered with arcane trinkets and tomes. Corin greeted her with a cautious smile, his silver hair pulled back into a loose braid.

"You're looking for Tavik Ryn?" Corin asked, cutting straight to the point as they sat in a backroom lined with enchanted wards.

Rowan nodded. "He's tied to something big and dangerous. What do you know?"

Corin hesitated, his fingers brushing against a black crystal on the table. "I've heard he's buying up rare components. Bloodstones, soul-binding chains, nightshade dust, an athame, pentacle… items commonly used in rituals that deal with death or worse–soul manipulation. Rowan, whatever he's planning, it's not good."

Her stomach churned, but she kept her expression neutral. "Thanks, Corin. Stay out of sight, alright?"

Lucian's contact was not someone the others in the team entirely trusted, primarily because of his dangerous reputation. Rhys Vale was a vampire of significant age and a former associate of Lucian's from centuries past. While most vampires operated within their covens or under strict hierarchies, Rhys was a rogue, a shadowy figure who thrived in the criminal underworld. He had an unmatched network of informants, thanks to his penchant for dealing in secrets, blackmail, and blood debts.

Lucian arranged to meet Rhys in the private lounge of The Glass Thorn, an exclusive club in Redhaven known for its secrecy and discretion. The room was dimly lit, with velvet curtains drawn tight and an enchantment over the walls to prevent eavesdropping. Rhys was already waiting when Lucian arrived, reclining in a high-back leather chair, a glass of crimson liquid swirling in his hand. His pale, sharp features were framed by dark, shoulder-length hair, and his eyes gleamed with predatory amusement.

"Lucian," Rhys drawled, his voice smooth as silk. "I must admit, I was surprised to hear from you. It's been, what... a century since we last crossed paths? And now you seek me out. I'm flattered."

"I don't have time for games, Rhys," Lucian said, his tone icy as he took a seat across from him. "I need information."

Rhys arched an eyebrow and took a leisurely sip from his glass. "Ah, straight to business. Very well, tell me, what is it you seek?"

"Tavik Ryn," Lucian replied, his gaze piercing. "I need to know where he is and what he's up to."

The name seemed to pique Rhys's interest. He set his glass down and leaned forward slightly. "Tavik Ryn. A fascinating figure. I've heard his name whispered in certain circles lately. Dangerous circles. He's been quite…active in Redhaven."

"What do you know?" Lucian pressed, his patience wearing thin.

Rhys smirked. "He's been purchasing rare items–artifacts, scrolls, and magical components. But not just any kind. He's been looking for relics tied to blood magic and soul manipulation. Extremely volatile stuff. Things most people wouldn't dare touch, let alone seek out."

Lucian's jaw tightened. "Where is he getting these items?"

Rhy's smirk widened. "He is working with another broker, a dealer named Marlic who operates out of the lower tunnels beneath Redhaven." Marlic's been supplying Tavik with some rather unique items—things that could only come from ancient vaults or forbidden archives. It seems Tavik is assembling something… significant."

"What is he trying to do?" Lucian asked, though he suspected Rhys wouldn't have a clear answer.

Rhys chuckled softly, leaning back in his chair. "Ah, if only I knew. Tavik plays his cards close to his chest. But I can tell you this: he's not working alone. There's a network behind him—small, but incredibly efficient. And they're moving fast. Whatever he's planning, it's coming soon."

Lucian stood, his expression hard. "Where can I find Malric?"

Rhys raised a hand. "Not so fast, my old friend. Information like this doesn't come without a price."

Lucian's eyes narrowed. "Name it."

Rhys's smile turned predatory. "A favor. One to be called in at a time of my choosing. You owe me one already from Paris, if I recall."

"I didn't think you were keeping score," Lucian replied coldly.

"I always keep score," Rhys said, his voice soft but firm. "Do we have a deal?"

Lucian hesitated only briefly before nodding. "Fine. But if this information turns out to be false, you'll regret it."

Rhys chuckled as Lucian turned to leave. "Oh, Lucian, you wound me. When have I ever steered you wrong?"

As Lucian stepped out of The Glass Horn, he tried to reach Sera, but she was not picking up. Frustrated, Lucian headed back to the safe house, hoping she had already returned.

As Sera stepped into the shadowed corner of the packed marketplace, she felt the weight of eyes on her. Her back-alley contact, a reclusive information broker named Liora, was already waiting, leaning casually against a stack of crates. Liora was a fae with a knack for uncovering the secrets no one else could. Secrets often whispered in places angels like Sera would never dare tread. Sera narrowed her eyes. "I need to know more about Tavik Ryn. What else is he planning? And why does he care so much about this ritual?"

Liora smirked. "Always straight to the point with you, huh?" She gestured for Sera to come closer. "Here's what I've got: Tavik isn't just looking for supernatural leaders' blood. He's obsessed with balance—restoring some 'cosmic equilibrium.' But there's a catch. They're not just sacrificing leaders. They need something more…divine." Liora's sharp gaze flicks up to meet Sera's.

Sera's heart skipped a beat. "Divine? What do you mean?"

Liora hesitated, lowering her voice. "Angelic blood, Sera. Specifically, an angel's grace. Tavik believes it's the key to unlocking the true power of the ritual. And from what I've heard, he's been watching you for a while."

The words hit Sera like a physical blow. She tried to mask her panic, but Liora saw through her. "They're not going to stop, Sera. If you're their target, you need to be ready."

Sera took a step back, her wings threatening to manifest in her distress. "Why me? There are other angels out there–"

"Not like you," Liora interrupted, her tone grim. "You're fallen but not fully severed from the divine. That makes you a bridge–a perfect conduit between the mortal and the celestial. They don't just want you for your grace; they want you for who you are."

The realization struck Sera like Lightning: Tavik Ryn and the Ascendants weren't just trying to complete a ritual–they were trying to rewrite the rules of existence itself, using her as the lynchpin. Without another word, Sera bolted from the meeting, the air crackling faintly as her grace stirred within her.

Back at the safe house, the team gathered around a worn wooden table strewn with notes, maps, and hastily scribbled reports. The air was tense, heavy with the weight of what they'd learned.

Rowan replayed Corin's information, her voice steady despite the dark implications. "He's after black magic components. Powerful ones. Whatever ritual he's planning, it's not small-scale."

Lucian leaned against the wall, his sharp, angular face illuminated by the dim light of a single bulb overhead. "And the Abyssal Chalice is the perfect place to acquire those items," he mused, his voice low and cold. "I've been there before. It's crawling with the worst kind of people."

Cassian grunted in agreement. "Zarek mentioned it, too. Tavik's definitely been there."

"They don't just want supernatural blood," Sera said, her eyes blazing with fear and anger. "They need me. My grace. If they succeed…I don't know what will happen, but it'll be catastrophic."

The team fell into a stunned silence. Naomi finally spoke, her voice steely. "Then we make damn sure they don't get you. But we need to prepare for the worst."

As the team scrambled to adjust their plans, Sera couldn't shake the feeling that Tavik Ryn was already a step ahead–and that her existence might doom them all if they weren't careful.

Sera, ever the optimist in light of her current situation, leaned forward with a glimmer of determination in her eyes. "Then that's our next move. But we need to be careful. If Tavik is tied to the Ascendants, he's not working alone."

Naomi nodded, feeling a flicker of hope despite the danger ahead. "Good. We'll plan tonight and move at dawn. Whatever happens, we do this together." The team exchanged brief but resolute glances, the fractures in their unity mending as they prepared to face the impossible.

Before they could delve deeper into their plans, an urgent ping from the security console shattered the relative calm. Lucian moved swiftly to the screen, his crimson eyes narrowing as he scanned the alert.

"It's the Council Intelligence Team," he said, his voice light. "They raided our old command center."

Rowan's breath hitched, but Sera raised a hand to calm the group. "We're fine. We moved everything days ago. They won't find anything useful."

Just then, Sera got word from another one of her contacts.

"I need to meet with someone," Sera said to the team.

Naomi looked at her for a long moment before finally replying, "Go, but take Lucian with you."

Sera and Lucian stepped out into the cold night air, her breath forming faint clouds in the dim light of the moon. They made their way to a secluded park on the outskirts of Redhaven, where she'd arranged to meet Calen, a male elf and former Council scout. She'd saved his life during a raid gone wrong, and he'd never forgotten it.

Calen appeared from the shadows, his lean frame wrapped in a dark cloak. "Sera," he greeted, his voice soft but laced with urgency. "What do you need?" He gave Lucian a long, judging look of disapproval. "I heard the human had formed a team of supernaturals, but I didn't want to believe she had included a blood sucker," Lucian smirked, showing his fangs.

"The CIT raid," she said bluntly. "What were their orders?"

He hesitated, glancing around to ensure they weren't being watched. "They're looking for evidence linking you to the Ascendants. The Council is nervous. They've been issuing new directives, but no one's allowed to question them. It's...strange."
"Strange how?"

"Like they're covering something up. I'll dig deeper, but you need to stay ahead of them. They've got more teams mobilizing."

Sera nodded, her mind already spinning with possibilities. "Thank you, Calen. Be careful."

When Sera and Lucian returned to the safe house, the team was waiting. She relayed Calen's intel, and the atmosphere grew even more tense.

"The Council is scared," Rowan said, her voice laced with suspicion. "Scared enough to send scouts after us. What aren't they telling us?"

"Doesn't matter," Cassian rumbled. "We stick to the plan. Find Tavik, stop whatever he's doing, and dismantle the Ascendants."

Lucian's lips curved into a sly smile, his fangs catching the light. "Agreed. And if the Council gets in our way, we deal with them too."

Still, the realization that the Council was actively hunting them left an uneasy silence in the room. The implications were clear: the Council was either desperate to control the situation, or they were hiding something. The team nodded, united in their purpose. Their priority had shifted for the moment. The Central Command vault would have to wait. With this new intel, the hunt for Tavik Ryn was on, and nothing—not the Ascendants, not the Council, and certainly not the shadows of Redhaven—would stop them.

Chapter 12

Breaking Tavik Ryn

The tension in the air was palpable as the team reconvened around the dimly lit table in their safehouse. Naomi leaned forward, her fingers pressed against a map spread across the wooden surface. Sera, her angelic grace hidden behind calm composure, stood at her side, her ethereal presence felt even in silence. Rowan fiddled with a rune-carved pendant, muttering to herself. Lucian leaned against the far wall as usual, scanning the room for any sign of doubt. Cassian paced restlessly, his heightened senses attuned to every creak of the old warehouse.

'We've got a lead on Tavik Ryn," Naomi announced, her voice firm but laced with urgency. "According to our informant, he's holed up in an abandoned cathedral outside the city. The place is crawling with Ascendant enforcers. If we're going in, we need to be ready to fight."

Sera's silver eyes flickered with a light that seemed otherworldly. "The Ascendants won't give him up easily. Tavik is their key to something bigger, something darker. We need to extract him and find out what he knows."

Cassian growled low, his claws extending for a moment before he reined himself in. "Let's not waste time, then. I've been itching for a good fight."

Rowan smirked. "Typical werewolf. Just don't get yourself killed, Cassian. I'd hate to waste a resurrection spell on you."

Lucian stepped forward, his voice cold and measured. "This isn't just a fight. It's a trap waiting to be sprung. We go in smart, or we don't come out at all."

With the location confirmed and the blueprints studied, the team was ready to make their move. Naomi devised a meticulous plan to infiltrate the foundry. Rowan and Sera would dismantle the outer wards, using Rowan's magic and Sera's celestial grace to avoid triggering the alarms.

Cassian and Lucian would create a distraction on the ground floor, drawing the attention of the enforcers while Naomi led the main assault team through the second floor. Vorlan had agreed to loan some of his most trusted guards to the team for this assault. Naomi would personally lead the charge to capture Tavik, ensuring no escape routes were left unchecked.

As the team prepared for the mission, the weight of what lay ahead was evident on each of their faces. Naomi glanced at the map one last time, her jaw set with determination. "This is it," she said. "We get Tavik, and we end this. No mistakes." The others nodded, their shared resolve visible. Whatever awaited them in the Ironclad Foundry, they would face it together.

Naomi nodded. "Then let's gear up. We move at Dawn."

Tavik Ryn's hideout was hidden deep in the industrial outskirts of Redhaven, the vast metropolis known for its blend of old-world architecture and modern decay. The area where he was said to be hiding was known as the Shattered Quarter, a section of the city abandoned decades ago after an industrial disaster left it riddled with toxins and crumbling buildings. Now, it served as a breeding ground for criminal activity, black-market dealings, and cult activity–the perfect cover for a figure like Tavik.

The team had spent days chasing fragmented clues about Tavik's location, following whispers through Redhaven's underbelly. Their break came from an unlikely source: a captured Ascendant deserter named Lirian Grey, who had once been Tavik's lieutenant.

During an interrogation led by Rowan and Lucian, Lirian had revealed critical information. Rowan had used a combination of potent truth spells and intimidation to pierce Lirian's defenses, while Lucian's icy demeanor left no room for negotiation. Ultimately, the deserter cracked, divulging that Tavik was hiding in an abandoned smelter plant on the outskirts of the Shattered Quarter.

Lirian claimed the smelter plant, formerly known as Ironclad Foundry, had been repurposed by the Ascendants into a fortress. He described its defenses in detail. Tavik had hired rogue mages to weave complex warding spells around the perimeter, making it nearly impossible to breach without setting off alarms. The foundry housed over two dozen Ascendant enforcers armed with dark artifacts, including cursed blades and explosive runes. It was also rumored to have a network of tunnels leading to Redhaven's sewer system, allowing Tavik to vanish if things went sideways.

Naomi, ever the strategist, had insisted on confirming the information before risking a raid. Sera and Rowan conducted reconnaissance using their unique skills. While cloaked in mortal form, Sera retained her angelic ability to sense disturbances in the spiritual energy. She detected a dense aura of malevolence radiating from the foundry, confirming it was a hub of dark activity.

Using a crystal pendulum and a scrying bowl filled with enchanted water, Rowan pinpointed Tavik's exact location within the foundry: an upper-level office used by factory supervisors, now converted into a command center for the Ascendants. He even provided blueprints of the foundry, stolen from the city archives, giving the team a critical advantage.

The ground floor of the foundry was a broad industrial complex with multiple levels, each designed for heavy manufacturing. A cavernous main hall filled with rusting machinery and conveyor belts. The space was patrolled by enforcers and rigged with magical tripwires designed to alert Tavik to intruders. The remains of molten slag pits were now used as holding cells for prisoners or sacrificial victims. Multiple side rooms contained caches of weapons and artifacts, presumably intended for the Ascendants' growing army.

The second-floor catwalks crisscrossed the smelter, providing high vantage points for sentries armed with crossbows enchanted to fire bolts and pure shadow. The control room, once used to monitor factory operations, had been converted into a war room filled with maps, Ascendant plans, and communication runes linking Tavik to other cult members.

The upper-level office was Tavik's personal quarters and command center. This was the old supervisor's office. The room had reinforced steel doors and was warded with protective spells. Inside, Tavik had amassed a trove of forbidden texts and artifacts, some of which even Sera would later recognize as remnants of celestial origin.

Beneath the foundry lay the escape tunnels Lirian had mentioned, though many were unstable due to decades of neglect. Rowan's divination revealed that Tavik had been stockpiling supplies there, anticipating the need for a swift retreat.

The abandoned cathedral looked like a specter on the horizon, its shattered stained-glass windows casting broken shards of light into the overgrown courtyard. The team approached cautiously, their weapons and abilities primed for battle.

Inside, the Ascendants waited. Clad in black robes and armed with enchanted weapons, they were fanatical and unyielding. The first wave struck as soon as the team breached the main doors. Rowan's spells erupted in flashes of fire and ice, while Lucian moved like a shadow, striking with lethal precision. Cassian tore through the ranks with raw, animalistic fury, his wolf form unleashed.

Naomi directed the chaos, her voice cutting through the noise like a blade. "Sera, cover the flank! Cassian, on me!"

But the Ascendants were more than foot soldiers. Their enforcers—elite warriors enhanced by dark magic—descended upon the team with ruthless efficiency. Sera, her celestial nature blazing to the surface, became their target.

A massive enforcer wielding a cursed sword charged at Naomi, who barely had time to react. Before the blow could land, Sera stepped in, her wings—brilliant and golden—unfurling in a burst of light. The enforcer's weapon shattered against her grace, but the effort drained her.

"You shouldn't have done that!" Naomi shouted, firing her pistol at another enemy.

"I will always protect you," Sera replied, her voice resonating with divine power.

But the Ascendants weren't finished. A surge of energy erupted from their leader, a powerful mage who commanded the dark forces binding the enforcers. The team began to falter, outnumbered and overwhelmed.

Then it happened. An enforcer hurled a dark spear of corrupted energy toward Rowan, who was too busy casting to see it coming. Without hesitation, Sera stepped into its path. The spear pierced her chest, and she fell to her knees, her light dimming.

"No!" Cassian's roar echoed through the cathedral as he tore through enemies to reach her.

Sera's grace flared one final time, creating a barrier of light that repelled the enforcers. "Go," she whispered. "I'll hold them off."

Naomi shook her head. "We're not leaving you!"

"You must. It's the only way," Sera said, her voice soft but unyielding.

As the team hesitated, a brilliant light descended from above. Divine angels, their forms radiant and blinding, appeared in defiance of their own laws. They encircled Sera, their voices a harmonious chorus.

"She has broken the covenant, but her sacrifice is pure," one chanted.

The light enveloped Sera, healing her wounds and lifting her to her feet. The divine angels vanished as quickly as they came, leaving the team stunned.

"There's no more time to question it," Lucian said. "We need to move!"

The Ascendants had retreated for now, but the cost of their victory weighed heavily. As the team delved deeper into their search for Tavik, they realized the cathedral was a maze of decay and forgotten grandeur. It stood in the heart of an overgrown graveyard, its crumbling facade a testament to years of neglect. Inside, however, the Ascendants had repurposed it into a stronghold of dark rituals and strategic operations. Tavik was hidden in the deepest recesses of the cathedral, surrounded by layers of traps, enforcers, and magical defenses.

The team had now entered the main hall, which was a cavernous space, its vaulted ceilings cloaked in the shadows. Dust motes swirled in the dim light cast by flickering braziers filled with eerie green flames. This was a trap. The Ascendants had placed magical tripwires disguised as broken pews and loose floor tiles, set to activate a swarm of defensive wards. Sera's celestial abilities allowed her to sense the malevolent energy in the air. She guided Rowan, who used precise counter-spells to disarm the magical triggers. As they moved cautiously through the hall, they encountered their second wave of resistance: guards armed with cursed crossbows and wielding jagged daggers inscribed with runes of binding. The fight was brutal and noisy, but the team prevailed, though they knew their presence had been revealed.

The real challenge lay beneath the cathedral. According to Rowan's divination, Tavik had established his hideout in the catacombs, an extensive network of tunnels and chambers beneath the main structure. These catacombs were initially meant to house the deceased clergy and their sacred relics, but the Ascendants had transformed them into a labyrinth of shadow and sorcery.

The team found the entrance to the catacombs concealed behind the altar in the cathedral's chancel. The altar had been desecrated, covered in dark sigils, and surrounded by the remains of the failed rituals. Cassian and Lucian worked together to move the heavy stone slab that concealed the entrance, revealing a spiral staircase that descended into the depths.

The catacombs were suffused with an oppressive energy. The air was cold, damp, and thick with the smell of decay. Rows of cracked stone coffins lined the walls, and ancient bones littered the floor. Rowan's magic lit the way with a faint golden glow, but the team remained on high alert as they navigated the narrow, twisting passageways.

Deep within the team came upon the Inner Sanctum, a vast, circular chamber lit by braziers burning with a strange, unnatural light. The walls were covered in intricate carvings that pulsed with dark energy, marking it as a place of significant power. At the center of the room stood Tavik Ryn, flanked by two elite Ascendant enforcers wielding enchanted spears. Tavik himself was tall and wiry, with hollow eyes and a face marked by years of obsession and corruption. He wore a dark, flowing robe inscribed with symbols, and around his neck hung a pendant that pulsed with an unsettling red light.

Tavik greeted the team with an air of defiance, his voice echoing ominously in the chamber. "So, you've finally come. I've been expecting you," he sneered, raising a hand to signal his enforcers. The fight was on. Rowan used her spells to neutralize Tavik's wards, opening a path for Cassian and Lucian to engage the enforcers in close combat. Tavik, however, wasn't defenseless. He wielded powerful dark magic, hurling bolts of shadow that forced the team to stay on the move constantly. Sera, despite the toll her earlier grace had taken, used her celestial light to protect the team from Tavik's most devastating attacks, her presence burning away the shadowy energy he conjured.

Naomi, ever the tactician, managed to flank Tavik while he was distracted. She fired a shot from her enchanted pistol, shattering the pendant around his neck. The artifact's destruction caused a ripple of destabilizing energy that stunned Tavik long enough for Lucian to pin him to the ground with preternatural speed.

With his enforcers defeated and his pendant destroyed, Tavik was at their mercy. Rowan wasted no time in binding him with enchanted chains that neutralized his magic. "You'll tell us everything," she hissed, her eyes blazing with determination. Tavik, bloodied but unbroken, gave a defiant laugh. "You think capturing me changes anything? You're already too late. The fallen will rise, and both Heaven and Earth will burn."

Tavik's command center was scattered with clues to the Ascendant's plans. There were several different maps of Redhaven marked with key locations, hinting at future attacks. Scrolls covered in incomprehensible runes, likely linked to the rituals they'd been performing, and a journal containing Tavik's notes, which would later prove invaluable.

The team dragged Tavik out of the sanctum and back through the cathedral, narrowly escaping as reinforcements began to flood in. By the time they emerged into the night air, battered and exhausted, the gravity of what they'd uncovered weighed heavily on all of them.

Tavik's cryptic warnings and the artifacts left behind in his sanctum hinted at a far greater danger than they'd anticipated. For now, though, they had their lead—and their prisoner.

The safehouse basement was dimly lit, the air thick with tension. Tavik sat bound to a chair, his wrists chained with enchanted silver that suppressed his magic. His face was pale, his breath uneven, but his defiant smirk remained. Tavik's screams echoed as Rowan and Lucian worked to extract the truth.

Naomi paced, her expression grim. Rowan, despite her formidable magical powers, recognized that extracting information from someone as dangerous and cunning as Tavik required more than just spells and threats. Tavik was no ordinary foe—he was a high-ranking member of the Ascendants, well-versed in counter magic and resistant to most conventional means of coercion. His mind was fortified not only by his dark magic but also by years of training to resist interrogation.

Tavik's mind was protected by a web of magical wards and mental barriers that Rowan's usual truth spells couldn't penetrate fully. These wards would actively resist any attempts to influence or compel him, causing a mental backlash to anyone attempting to break through them. Rowan could weaken the barriers with her magic, but doing so was risky and slow. She needed Lucian's vampiric powers to exploit the openings she created.

As a vampire, Lucian possessed the ability to dominate minds through a combination of hypnotic suggestion and supernatural charisma. This ability allowed him to bypass many of the natural defenses of the human mind, slipping past the cracks in Tavik's mental armor. While Tavik's magical wards were powerful, they were not designed to counter the unique predatory magic of a vampire.

Lucian's power wasn't just about forcing Tavik to speak—it was about subtly steering his thoughts and emotions, weakening his resolve without Tavik realizing it. Once Lucian established a foothold in Tavik's mind, he could pry loose the secrets that Tavik was desperate to hide.

Rowan and Lucian worked in tandem, their methods complementing each other. Rowan used her magic to dispel Tavik's mental wards, breaking down the magical protections that shielded his thoughts. She carefully dismantled these barriers layer by layer, ensuring that Tavik's mind didn't collapse completely–a state that would render him useless for interrogation. As Rowan weakened the barriers, Lucian stepped in, using his vampiric influence to probe Tavik's mind. He manipulated Tavik's emotions, drawing out his fear and paranoia to make him more susceptible to questioning.

Lucian's vampiric senses made him an invaluable interrogator. He could hear the subtle changes in Tavik's heartbeat, smell the shift in his pheromones, and detect even the slightest hesitation in his voice. This would allow him to instantly identify when Tavik was lying or withholding information, giving Rowan the ability to counter those lies with additional spells or questions.

Rowan circled him, her hands glowing faintly with magical energy. "You can make this easy, Tavik, or I can make it excruciating. Your choice."

Tavik chuckled, "You think you can break me, witch? I've endured worse than you could imagine."

Lucian stepped into the light, his crimson eyes gleaming like embers. His presence alone was enough to send a chill through Tavik's resolve. "Oh, I think you'll find her imagination is quite vivid," Lucian said smoothly, his voice low and hypnotic. "But I'm here to ensure she doesn't have to work too hard."

Rowan placed her hands on Tavik's temples, her magic flowing into his mind like tendrils of light. Tavik's smirk faltered as the barriers he'd built began to crack. "You're good," Rowan admitted, her voice calm but laced with irritation. "These wards are impressive, but they're not flawless."

Lucian leaned closer, his voice dropping to a whisper that seemed to echo in Tavik's mind. "Let her in, Tavik. You can feel it, can't you? The walls are crumbling. It's only a matter of time. Why prolong your suffering?"

Tavik's breath quickened, his confidence wavering. "You…you can't break me," he hissed, though the fear in his voice betrayed him.

Lucian's smile revealed his sharp fangs. "I don't need to break you. I just need to find the cracks."

As Rowan dismantled the last of the mental wards, Lucian's power surged. His voice became a commanding force, weaving through Tavik's mind and pulling forth the

secrets he so desperately tried to hide. Tavik gasped, his will crumbling under the combined assault of magic and vampiric dominance.

"You want to talk now," Lucian said, his tone both a statement and a compulsion. "You want to tell us everything, because you know there's no escape."

Sweat poured down Tavik's face as he began to speak, his words tumbling out in a mixture of fear and desperation.

"He's breaking," Rowan said, her voice cold. He revealed the Ascendants' plans, their leader's identity, and their ultimate goal: the unification of Heaven and Hell under the control of a fallen angel.

Finally, Tavik gasped, his resolve shattered. "The Ascendants' leader… he's a fallen angel, like your precious Sera," he spat.

What's his goal?' Naomi demanded.

"To tear down Heaven and Earth," Tavik sneered. "He wants revenge on both realms. And he's close to succeeding."

"How?" Sera's voice was sharp, her grace still flickering around her. She knew of only a few other fallen angels in Eterna besides herself.

Tavik smirked, blood staining his teeth. "There's a magical artifact. Once that holds the power to unite Heaven and Hell under his command. The Fragment of Faith. That's what he needs. And once he has it…"

By the end of the interrogation, Tavik was a broken man, his secrets laid bare. For a moment, the room was silent, save for Tavik's labored breathing. Rowan and Lucian's combined methods had not only extracted the truth but ensured that Tavik would never dare resist them again. Rowan turned to Lucian, a flicker of grudging respect in her eyes.

"Remind me never to get on your bad side," she said, her tone light but serious.

Lucian smirked. "I'll add it to the growing list of reasons."

The team exchanged grim looks as the weight of his words settled over them. The stakes had never been higher.

Naomi finally spoke, her voice steely. "We're going to stop him. Whatever it takes."

The maps on the table once more, a new location marked–a place where the Fragment of Faith was said to be hidden, as well as Tavik's journal proving their mission was far from over, and the cost of failure was unimaginable.

Chapter 13

Fracture of Power

Darkness draped the street of Redhaven, where the dim glow of neon reflected off the glistening wet asphalt. Central Command stood in the heart, a monolithic fortress of glass and steel. It was where Naomi, Rowan, and Lucian were headed while Sera and Cassian split off to make a quick stop at her contact's location.

Naomi led the team toward Central Command, her gear pristine and utilitarian. Rowan adjusted the intricate silver runes sewn in her cloak, her delicate hands glowing faintly with pre-cast protection spells. Lucian followed with predatory grace, his eyes scanning every shadow as if danger itself might be hiding there. The three disappeared around the corner, their mission clear: to strategize and prepare for the inevitable confrontation. The group's synchronized efforts marked the culmination of months of investigation and planning, each moment more critical than the last.

The air was damp as Cassian and Sera weaved through the back alleys. Their mission was different more delicate, and, in some ways, far more dangerous. They were heading to meet one of Sera's old contacts, a figure who thrived in the underground world of celestial secrets and forbidden knowledge. Cassian's sharp ears caught every scuffle of a rat's paw or distinct shout, but his focus remained on Sera. Her wings were tucked close to her sides, the feathers bristling subtly, ready to spring into action at the slightest hint of danger. Cassian could feel the weight of her presence, both ethereal and commanding.

The meeting was arranged in an old, weathered building at the edge of the Crescent Quarter, the district known for its blend of vibrant culture within the supernatural community. The once-glorious structure was now a shell of its former self, riddled with graffiti, overgrown vines, and rust-laden metal doors with bars on broken stained-glass windows. Moonlight filtered through the jagged glass, casting eerie shadows across the structure.

Cassian, his tense frame, stood protectively beside Sera. His leather jacket and combat boots made him look more like a brawler than a member of the elite task force. His sharp eyes flicked to every corner of the alley, his senses on high alert.

"Are you sure about this?" He murmured, his deep voice barely audible.

"Are you sure your contact will even talk?" Cassian asked, his voice low.

Sera shot him a sidelong glance, her eyes cold yet uncertain. "I trust him. Or, at least, I trust that his self-interest aligns with ours for now."

Sera rapped on the door in a sequence: three quick knocks, a pause, then two more. A slit in the door opened, revealing a pair of amber eyes. "Password."

"Redemption is a lie," Sera said flatly. The slit closed, and the door creaked open.

Inside, the building was a stark contrast to its exterior. Brightly lit monitors and

holographic screens dominated the room, while servers hummed along the walls. At the center sat a slender man with pale, almost ethereal features. His stark white hair fell around his face in messy waves, and his violet eyes gleamed with an unnatural intelligence. He wore a mismatched ensemble of a tailored waistcoat over a threadbare coat, giving him the look of a fallen aristocrat.

"Kade," Sera said, her voice neutral but guarded. "Still holed up in places like this, I see."

Kade offered a sly smile, his voice like silk. "And you, dear Sera, still consorting with mortals and beasts, I see. How quaint." His gaze found Cassian, who growled low in his throat but held his ground.

"Enough games," Sera snapped, her tone sharp. "I need information, and I know you have it."

Kade's smirk widened. "I might know a few things, but this time, the price is higher. You know how dangerous it is to poke around in matters of the Divine."

Sera's jaw tightened. She knew exactly what he was talking about. Despite her disgrace, she still felt their shadow looming over her every step. They had intervened and saved her from death at the foundry.

"I'll pay it," she said firmly. Though Casian glanced at her with concern.

Kade chuckled, leaning casually in his chair. "Very well. You're looking into another fallen one, aren't you? Not one of yours, though."

"Who is he?" Sera demanded.

Kade's expression shifted, a glimmer of genuine unease crossing his face. "He calls himself Azareth."

Sera frowned. "I've never heard of him."

"That's because he was exiled long before your fall, Sera. Azareth was one of the first to defy Heaven, not out of rebellion, but ambition. He believed he could ascend to godhood himself. When he failed, Heaven erased him from history. Only those of us who were there remember."

"And now he's leading the Ascendants," Cassian muttered.

Kade gestured to the screens, pulling up a digital projection of an ancient artifact. "The Fragment of Faith," he said, his voice heavy with irony. "A fragment of the celestial gate that once connected Heaven to Earth. If he completes his collection of artifacts, he could open the gate and challenge Heaven's dominion."

Kade hesitated, then typed rapidly. A map of Redhaven appeared, zooming in on a derelict part of the city near the docks. "Here. But you're not the only ones looking for it." Sera's mind raced.

The room fell silent as his words hung in the air. Even Cassian, usually skeptical of celestial drama, looked troubled.

"You know what this means, don't you?" Kade said, his voice quieter now. "If he succeeds, it's not just Heaven or Hell that will fall. It's everything."

Sera clenched her fists, her mind reeling. For centuries, she'd believed she was untethered from the Divine, that her fall had severed her from them. But now, it seemed she'd been pulled back into a game far bigger than herself.

Kade straightened, his smirk returning as if to dispel the weight of his words. "Well, that's all you're getting from me. For now, at least. Be careful, Sera, Azareth isn't the kind of enemy you can face unprepared."

As Kade left the room, Cassian turned to Sera, his expression grim. "This Azareth… what do we do about him?"

Sera's dark eyes gleamed with a mix of determination and fear. "We find him before he finds us. And we make damn sure we're ready for his plan."

With that, they left the building, the moonlight guiding their way as they headed toward Central Command to meet the rest of the team.

Meanwhile, across the city, Naomi crouched behind the dense underbrush near the eastern perimeter, her hand gripping the comms device clipped to her ear. The map provided by Councilor Vorlan was spread out in her mind, its lines etched with precision from hours of planning. She glanced at Rowan, who knelt beside her, murmuring faint incantations under her breath; the faint glow of her magic was dull enough to blend with the ambient shadows.

"Outer security grid is down," Rowan whispered, her voice carrying a calm confidence. "Your turn, Naomi."

Naomi nodded and activated the code sequence that Vorlan had provided. The security system flickered briefly, the shimmering energy shields dissipating just enough for them to slip through. Rowan straightened, her sharp eyes narrowing as she assessed the patrol patterns ahead.

"Move now," Naomi ordered, her voice low but resolute.

Lucian and Cassian emerged from the shadows behind them, making no sound as they fell into formation. Lucian's gaze flickered with amusement, as if Cass were ready to spring into action at the slightest provocation, his muscles taut with barely restrained energy.

Sera had taken up a position further north, prepared to serve as both lookout and distraction if needed. The fallen angel's presence was like a whisper of a storm, her power muted but ever-present, a reminder of what was at stake should they fail tonight.

Naomi crouched low, her dark armor blending seamlessly with the shadows of Central Command. Rowan's enchantments masked their presence, rendering them undetectable to sensors and patrols. Lucian moved ahead, his senses attuned to every shift in the air.

The maps and codes provided by Vorlan had proven invaluable. Naomi led them through a maze of corridors, bypassing locked doors and evading patrols with precision. As they moved deeper into the facility, the team operated like ghosts. Rowan's magic cloaked their movements, masking their footsteps and silencing the faint hum of Lucian's preternatural speed. Cassian moved with surprising grace for someone his size, his instincts allowing him to sense and avoid patrols before they even came into view.

Naomi held up a hand, signaling for the team to halt. They had reached the hub, where the vault was located. The door to the vault loomed ahead, an imposing slab of reinforced steel inscribed with glyphs that glowed faintly in the dim light.

Rowan stepped forward, her fingers brushing over the runes. "Anti-tampering wards," she murmured, her voice smooth and low. "Clever, but not clever enough."

"Can you disarm them?" Naomi asked.

"With Lucian's help, easily. I'll need his power."

Lucian joined her, his hands joining hers in practiced motions as she muttered a spell. The air grew heavy, and the runes began to flicker and dim. After a tense moment, the glow faded entirely, and Lucian stepped back with satisfaction.

"After you," he said, gesturing to Naomi.

She approached the keypad beside the vault door, entering the first combination from Tavik's journal. The lock clicked, and the door slid open with a hiss, revealing rows of deposit boxes lining the walls. Each box was marked with a sigil, the artifacts within pulsing faintly with energy.

"Take everything," Naomi ordered, her voice steady despite the rush of adrenaline coursing through her veins.

The team worked quickly, using the combinations from the journal to open the boxes. Rowan conjured a series of containment wards to prevent the artifacts from reacting violently to their removal. Lucian moved with supernatural speed, opening each box and retrieving the artifacts: a golden chalice, a fragment of celestial armor, and an ancient scroll etched with symbols that glowed faintly. Each item pulsed with divine energy, the power almost overwhelming. Cassian stood guard at the entrance, his senses on high alert for any sign of approaching danger.

"Got them," Lucian said, his voice tight.

"Let's move," Naomi ordered. They slipped back out the same way they came, the vault sealing behind them. Not a single alarm sounded, and the guards remained oblivious.

Chapter 14

The Fragment of Faith

The team stood just beyond the wrought-iron gates of Central Command, the shadows of the tall spires stretching across the cracked cobblestones. Noami unfolded the map, the edges worn and frayed with age. Sera's luminous gaze lingered on the map's intricate markings, her feathered wings shimmering faintly in the moonlight. Beside her, Rowan adjusted her satchel of enchanted tools, the silver sigils embroidered on her cloak glinting as they caught the light. Lucian stood a few paces away, his eyes scanning their surroundings with predatory precision. Cassian, with his perpetual aura of energy, shifted restlessly, his senses undoubtedly alert to every sound and scent in the wind.

Naomi traced her finger over the map. Her voice was steady despite the weight of their mission. "The docks," she said, pointing to an area marked with swirling sigils and ancient runes. "This is where the Fragment of Faith is hidden. The cult must already be there, and Azareth won't be far behind."

Sera nodded, her expression serene yet resolute. "The Fragment's presence will distort the veil between realms. We'll feel it the closer we get, but so will Azareth."

Rowan muttered an incantation under her breath, her hand brushing the protective charms at her belt. "This part of the city is crawling with dark energy. It's not just the cult we need to worry about; the Shards' power could have awakened all kinds of things."

The group set off, navigating the labyrinth of streets that stretched before them like a tangled web. The air grew heavier with each step, a mix of salt from the nearby sea and the acrid stench of decay. This part of the city, known as the Black Harbor District, had long been abandoned. Once a bustling hub of trade and commerce, it had fallen into ruin decades after the great flood. The flood waters had receded, but the damage remained – A network of skeletal buildings leaning precariously, their windows shattered and walls cloaked in moss and creeping ivy.

The streets were eerily silent, except for the occasional drip of water echoing from rusted pipes and the distant creak of a ship's mast. Street lights, dim and flickering, seemed to float in the air, casting an otherworldly glow. Shadows danced in the corners of their vision, but whether they were tricks of the light or something more sinister, none of them could say.

"We're close," Naomi whispered, her voice barely audible over the sound of their footsteps. She glanced up, her eyes narrowing as she spotted a towering structure at the edge of the district. It was an old church, its spire bent and broken, the stone facade marred with deep cracks. The building leaned toward the sea as if bowing to the inevitability of its collapse. According to the map, the Fragment of Faith was hidden beneath the church, in the crypts that had been sealed for centuries.

"Lovely place," Lucian remarked dryly, his voice laced with sarcasm. He adjusted the collar of his coat, his fangs briefly glinting as he smirked. "Nothing like a little desecration to hide a celestial artifact."

Cassian snorted, his sharp canines flashing as he grinned. "Maybe you can chat up a ghost or two while we're here."

"Focus," Naomi said firmly, cutting off their banter. "The cult will have guards, traps, and possibly worse. We need to stick together."

The team navigated the docks, the air thick with salt and the smell of oil. The area was desolate, with abandoned factories and shipping containers rusting in the moonlight. Shadows danced across the cracked pavement, cast by flickering floodlights.

As they approached the church, Sera's wings fluttered slightly, the Golden glow around her intensifying. "The Fragment is close," she said, her voice carrying a note of urgency. " I can feel its pull. But there's something else… a darkness clinging to it. Azareth's taint, no doubt."

Rowan knelt by the church's entrance, her fingers tracing the runes carved into the ancient wood of the door. "This isn't just an ordinary seal," she murmured. "It's a ward—one that repels divine and infernal energy. Sera, Lucian, you'll need to hang back while I dismantle this."

Lucian scoffed, leaning casually against the crumbling stone wall. "Take your time, Row. I'll just be over here… not getting incinerated."

Sera folded her arms, her expression patient but firm. "The Fragment is more important than your pride, Lucian. Let Rowan work."

Naomi scanned their surroundings as Rowan worked, her hand resting on the hilt of her sword. The streets were too quiet, the shadows too still. "Cassian, do you smell anything?"

Cassian's nostrils flared as he tilted his head, his eyes narrowing. "Blood," he growled, his voice low and dangerous. "Fresh. And it's not human."

"This place feels wrong," Sera muttered, her hand on the hilt of her dagger.

Lucian scanned the surroundings. "It's quiet. Too quiet."

The group tensed, weapons at the ready. Moments later, a low, guttural growl echoed from the darkness, followed by the scrape of claws on stone. The cult wasn't the only danger lurking in the Black Harbor District, and as the first of the shadowy figures emerged from the gloom, the air grew sick with the promise of violence.

"Whatever it is, it's not here to help us," Naomi said grimly, drawing her blade. "Rowan, how much longer?"

"Just a few more seconds!" Rowan called, her voice taut with concentration as she dismantled the ward.

Lucian stepped forward, his fangs bared and eyes blazing. "Then let's make those seconds count."

The first creature lunged from the shadows, a mass of sinewy limbs and serrated claws. Its eyes, black voids, locked onto Naomi as it screeched– a sound like rusted metal scraping against stone. Naomi barely had time to raise her sword before it was upon her.

She sidestepped, twisting her blade upward in a practiced arc. The steel met flesh, cutting deep, but the creature barely flinched. Its thick hide absorbed the blow, and it retaliated with a swipe of jagged claws. Naomi ducked, the wind of its attack brushing past her cheek, and drove her blade forward, aiming for its throat.

To her left, Cassian roared, his form shifting mid-air as he leaped at another beast. Bones cracked, fur sprouted, and within seconds, the man was gone, replaced by a massive werewolf with golden eyes burning like embers. He met the creature's charge head-on, their bodies colliding with a sickening crunch. Fangs tore into flesh, claws raked across muscle, but Cassian's raw strength won out as he slammed the beast to the ground, his jaws snapping around its throat.

Lucian moved like a shadow, one moment standing still, the next disappearing in a blur. He reappeared behind a second beast, his eyes glowing as his fangs pierced its neck. The creature shrieked, its body writhing as Lucian drained its essence, its very life force slipping into his grasp. He let the lifeless husk fall, licking the blood from his lips with a smirk.

Sera, her wings flaring with divine radiance, faced a monstrosity with elongated limbs and spines protruding from its back. The creature lunged, but she lifted her hands, and golden chains of celestial light erupted from her palms, wrapping around the abomination like a vice. It howled, its skin blistering where the divine shackles burned, and Sera's voice rang out like a bell in the night. "You were never meant to walk this world." With a final gesture, the chains tightened, and the creature shattered into nothing but dust.

Rowan, standing behind the group, murmured an incantation, her hands tracing sigils in the air. The runes on her cloak ignited with violet energy, and suddenly, a barrier of flickering light erupted between the team and the remaining creatures.

"Move!" she shouted. "I can't hold them forever!"

Naomi, Cassian, Lucian, and Sera regrouped, cutting down the last of the beasts as Rowan's barrier wavered. The final creature, massive, with a gaping mouth lined with too many teeth, snarled and lunged at Rowan. Before it could reach her, Cassian barreled into its side, sending it crashing into the church wall. Lucian finished it off with a precise thrust of his blade, piercing through its skull. The street fell silent, except for the heavy breathing of the team. The battle was over, but the true challenge was waiting inside.

The church now loomed before them, its stone walls worn by time and decay. The heavy wooden doors creaked open, revealing a vast, dust-choked chamber illuminated only by the fractured moonlight streaming through stained-glass windows. The air smelled of mildew and forgotten prayers.

"This place is ancient," Rowan murmured, running her fingers over the worn engravings on the nearest pillar. "The passage to the crypts should be hidden somewhere in the sanctuary."

Lucian sniffed the air, his senses sharp. "We don't have much time. Azareth is close."

Naomi led the way down the middle, the others fanning to search. Sera stepped near the altar, her fingers grazing the intricate carvings along its base. "These markings… they're not just decorative." She traced the grooves with her hand, and suddenly, the floor beneath them rumbled.

Stone groaned as a hidden mechanism engaged, and part of the floor near the altar slid away, revealing a dark staircase spiraling into the depths of the earth.

Naomi drew her sword. "This is it."

Without hesitation, they descended into the crypts, the air growing colder with each step. The torches lining the walls flickered, their flames barely clinging to life. The weight of centuries pressed upon them as they reached the bottom-a vast chamber lined with stone sarcophagi.

They found the Fragment in the center of the room, encased in an obsidian pedestal. The fragment glowed faintly, its energy resonating through the air. Naomi approached cautiously, her hand outstretched. The Fragment of Faith pulsed with ethereal light.

"Wait," Rowan warned, her voice sharp. "It's warded."

Lucian stepped forward, his fangs bared. "Let me handle it."

But they weren't alone. Before he could act, the shadows around them shifted, and figures emerged: The cultists emerged from the shadows, their robes the color of dried blood and their faces obscured by masks. At their center stood a towering figure, his wings black as midnight, his once-divine form corrupted by centuries of exile. His gaze, burning with malice, locked onto the team.

"Azareth," Sera whispered, her voice barely audible.

The fallen angel smiled, his presence suffocating. "You've done well to come this far. But you're too late, the Fragment belongs to me."

The team tightened their formation, weapons drawn. Naomi met Azareth's gaze, unflinching. "Not today."

Lucian smirked. "You'll have to kill us first."

Azareth raised his hand, and the crypt erupted into chaos.

The cultists attacked first, their daggers gleaming in the dim light. Naomi met them head-on, her sword cutting through the first assailant with deadly precision. Cassian tore through another, his claws raking through flesh. Sera took to the air, her wings a blur as she unleashed spears of divine energy, striking down any who dared approach.

Rowan chanted a powerful spell, summoning chains of violet fire that wrapped around two cultists, incinerating them where they stood. But Azareth was undeterred.

With a single gesture, he sent a shockwave through the chamber, knocking them back. He advanced on the Shard, but Lucian intercepted him, his speed barely keeping him ahead of the fallen angel's attacks. Their blades clashed, sparks flying, but Azareth was stronger. He hurled Lucian into a stone pillar with enough force to crack the ancient structure.

Sera descended, blocking Azareth's path. "You were once an angel," she said, her voice steady. "You don't have to do this."

Azareth sneered. "I was cast down. Forgotten. I will take my place among the gods once more."

He struck, but Sera met his attack, the force of their collision shaking the chamber. Naomi and Cassian leapt in, their combined assault forcing Azareth back. Rowan, still standing by the Shard, began working on the protective wards binding it.

Lucian staggered to his feet, his gaze locking onto Rowan. "Hurry."

"I'm trying!" she shot back, her fingers weaving through the ancient symbols.

Azareth, enraged, sent another shockwave through the chamber. The ceiling cracked, and dust and stone rained down. "You will not take what is mine!" he roared.

But Sera, battered and bloodied, surged forward, her sword glowing with celestial energy. With a final, desperate strike, she drove her blade through Azareth's chest. The fallen angel gasped, his wings fading. His body fluttered between realms before he let out a final, agonized cry—and then he was gone, his form disintegrating into nothing. The remaining cultists, seeing their leader vanquished, fled into the darkness.

Rowan and Lucian finished breaking the wards, and the Fragment of Faith dimmed, its energy settling. The battle was over. The team, barely standing, emerged from the crypts, the weight of their victory settling upon them.

"That was too close," Cassian muttered, wiping blood from his brow.

Lucian exhaled sharply, glancing at Rowan. "Nice work, Row."

Rowan smirked despite the exhaustion. "Told you I could handle it."

Sera looked toward the horizon, where dawn was beginning to break. "We have what we came for."

Naomi took a deep breath, gripping the fragment tightly. "Then let's get out of here."

Chapter 15

Corruption In High Places

The battle was over. Azareth was dead. The cult that had nearly torn Eterna apart had scattered like leaves in a storm, leaderless and broken. Yet, as Naomi stood outside the ruined church, dust still clinging to her skin and exhaustion weighing on her bones, she knew this was far from over.

The others were in similar states–Sera's glow was dimmed, Rowan's usually sharp gaze was dulled by fatigue, Cassian nursed a wound on his arm that had barely begun to close, and Lucian, ever composed, had his eyes narrowed in deep thought.

Just then, the radio on Naomi's belt crackled to life.

"Chancellor Velthara Stormveil to Team Omega. Report back to Central Command immediately." The Chancellor's voice was sharp, clipped, and angry. "We have a developing situation. Councilor Vorlan has brought something to my attention that demands immediate investigation."

Naomi exchanged glances with her team before responding. "Understood, Chancellor. We're on our way."

Sera exhaled a slow breath, her wings twitching slightly. "Something tells me this isn't over."

"It never is," Lucian murmured, adjusting his coat.

With the church crumbling behind them, the team disappeared into the city, the Fragment of Faith secured, but knowing this was not over.

Chancellor Stormveil was waiting for them the moment they arrived at Central Command. The grand hall of the government complex was nearly empty at this late hour, except for the guards stationed along the massive stone pillars. The Chancellor's silver hair was pulled back tightly, and her storm-grey eyes carried the weight of barely restrained fury.

"You're here," she said curtly, motioning them forward into her private chamber.

The moment the doors closed behind them, she dropped an envelope onto the table. "Do you want to know what I just learned?" she asked, voice deceptively calm.

No one answered, waiting for her to continue.

"Councilor Vorlan met with me right after Lord Merrick's murder. He claimed several of my Councilors were conspiring behind my back to overthrow the current government and reshape Eterna. It has now been confirmed that Azareth was not acting alone, not entirely in this conspiracy." She turned to Naomi. "So, I personally searched Merrick's chambers and found a couple of things. There was a false bottom in his desk drawer. Inside was a journal. I also found a hidden camera as well," she said as she slid the envelope across the table toward Naomi.

As the team gathered around the table, Naomi passed the journal to Lucian and began to load the video surveillance onto the laptop. What they began to piece together based on the intel from both was astonishing.

Lord Merrick had never feared the dark. He had presided over Eterna's highest court for three decades, passing judgment on criminals, corrupt officials, and conspirators alike. Justice was his creed, and he wielded it without bias, earning him both deep respect and bitter enemies. But as he sat alone in his chambers at Eclipse Hall on the night of his murder, he was beginning to feel something he had never experienced before–genuine fear.

Days earlier, he had stumbled upon something he was never meant to see. It had started with a simple curiosity: irregularities in financial records tied to the Council's discretionary funds. What had first seemed like a bureaucratic oversight quickly unraveled into something more sinister. Hidden among routine transactions were coded payments–diverted resources sent to shell organizations that, when traced, led back to none other than the now-dead cult leader Azareth.

Merrick had followed the trail with the tenacity of a man who had dedicated his life to exposing corruption. But as he pieced together the evidence, it became clear that some of Eterna's most powerful figures were involved. He had planned to bring the matter to Chancellor Stormveil the next morning, but the cult had other plans.

That night, as he prepared his case, a whisper of movement in the darkness of his chambers was the only warning he received. The assassin struck with precision–a dream piercer blade, infused with dark magic, piercing through his heart before he could so much as rise from his desk.

By dawn, Merrick was found sprawled across his desk, blood pooling across the damning evidence he had gathered. The documents were gone.

Chancellor Stormveil explained that when Vorlan reached out, she acted immediately. With the team's investigation into the cult already in motion, she knew she needed a second force—one that could work in the shadows to uncover who had murdered Merrick and why.

She had called upon a select few: operatives trained for the most dangerous and covert missions. These were good soldiers, spies, and investigators who answered only to her. They would go where no one else could, and they would not stop until the truth was unearthed.

The Special Ops team she selected was Eterna's best. In charge was Commander Riven Duskbane, a master strategist and seasoned field operative. Riven had hunted war criminals in the borderlands. He was relentless, calculating, and loyal only to Stormveil's vision of a just Eterna. His right-hand gal, Major Veyra Kallus, was a shadow dancer who was trained in the ancient arts of espionage. She could move unseen, slipping past wards and locked doors with an ease that defied reason. Next up was Jorek Blackwell, a former investigator from Eterna's Watch, now an expert interrogator and forensic specialist. His methods were ruthless, but they got results. Finishing up the team was Talon

Varros, a sharpshooter and tracker with an eye for patterns. If there were a trail, he would find it.

Riven began updating the team on the Ops part of the investigation. Their mission had been clear: Find out who killed Merrick, recover the stolen documents, and expose the conspiracy he had uncovered before his death. The investigation led them first to Eclipse Hall.

Blackwell had examined the murder scene meticulously. It was a clean kill. There was no hesitation in the wound. It wasn't a message—it was an execution. Veyra had run her fingers along the edges of a hidden compartment in Merrick's desk.

She deduced he knew he was in danger. He had been hiding something, and whatever it was, the killer had taken it. Riven had surveyed the chamber. They all knew Merrick was no fool. If he had suspected something this big, he wouldn't have put all his trust in a single set of documents. There would've been copies. They had checked his records and contacts and looked around to see if he had left any other clues behind.

While the rest of the team was examining Merrick's chamber, Talon had worked on the external security feeds. Most had been wiped, but a few frames had remained. The frames showed a robed figure slipping past the Hall's security defenses. The robe had the sigil of a cult, which they later identified as Azareth's based on what Naomi's team had uncovered. All the intel collected had confirmed that Merrick had found something damning enough for the cult to risk breaking into one of the most secure places in Eterna just to silence him.

Naomi's team exchanged glances. It was a lot for each of them to process, not knowing there had been a coinciding investigation they were not aware of.

"How high does this go?" Naomi asked. Chancellor Stormveil's expression darkened. "I want you to find out. I am merging Ops with your team. I am officially ordering an investigation into this conspiracy. If Vorlan is right, we may be dealing with a level of corruption unlike anything seen in Eterna's history."

"I need names," Stormveil continued. "I need proof, and I need this rot excised from the heart of our government before it festers any further. Do whatever it takes, but be discreet. If they realize we're onto them, they'll bury their tracks."

She didn't need to say more. As they left the chamber, the echoes of her orders were still lingering in the air. The rest of the team had stepped away to prepare, but the two commanders remained behind, knowing a decision had to be made.

Riven had leaned against the stone wall, arms crossed, his expression unreadable. He had led the Special Ops team through the Merrick investigation, but now their missions were merging. Two very different squads, one objective.

Naomi met his gaze, her posture firm. "This is going to get messy. We need a clear chain of command."

Riven nodded, exhaling slowly. "And that should be you."

Naomi raised an eyebrow. "That easy?"

He smirked, shaking his head. "I know my strengths, and I know yours. You've been running point on Azareth and the cult since the beginning. You have the full picture, the momentum. My team was chasing a single thread–yours has been untangling the entire web." He pushed off the wall, standing straight. "I don't have an ego about this. The mission is what matters, and you're the best one to lead it."

Naomi studied him for a moment, searching for any hint of reluctance. She found none—just pragmatism and trust.

"Then I'll take the lead," she said. "But I'll need your insight. You know the players we're dealing with better than anyone."

Riven gave a short nod. "Consider me your second. I'll run support and keep my team in line." His smirk returned. "Not that they need much handling–Veyra would kill me in my sleep if I micromanaged."

Naomi chuckled. "Sounds like Rowan."

A moment of mutual respect passed between them before Riven extended a hand. "Let's finish this."

Naomi clasped his forearm. "Together."

Chapter 16

Unraveling The Web

The halls of Merrick Manor were eerily silent as Naomi and her team moved through its grand corridors. Chandeliers hung above them, swaying ever so slightly, casting fractured light against the gilded walls. The air smelled of aged wood and something faintly metallic–blood, long since cleaned but never truly erased. Lord Merrick's murder had shaken the city's political core, and Chancellor Stormveil had made it clear the teams' directive. The deeper the team dug, the more tangled the web of deceit had become.

Jorek & Talon had started gathering all of his staff while others were searching the manor. Riven stood beside Naomi, arms crossed, his sharp eyes scanning the hall's towering bookshelves as if expecting secrets to lurk in the very architecture. The rest of the team had spread out, going from room to room. It didn't take long for something unusual to come to light.

Rowan, poring over spell-marked parchments, muttered under her breath. "This isn't just bribery. There's blood magic in some of these contracts. Ritualistic bindings." She tapped a finger against the faded sigils. "Someone's been using old magic to enforce obedience." The documents found in Merrick's study revealed questionable transactions–large sums of money funneled into ghost companies with no discernible purpose. Upon further digging, Rowan's magic uncovered hidden seals within the pages, revealing something even more insidious.

"They were paying people off," Rowan murmured, tracing the sigils with her fingers. "Blackmail. Bribes. Assassinations."

The city was in chaos. The more they uncovered, the deeper the corruption ran. But one thing was certain–Merrick had tried to expose them and paid the ultimate price.

Until recently, Azareth had been a ghost, a myth whispered in the dark. But now, it was undeniably clear–he had been orchestrating this corruption. His influence had seeped into the highest ranks, manipulating every level of the city.

It had begun with whispers. A missing ledger here, a bribed official there. But as the investigation gained momentum, the true scale of the deception unfolded like a plague-ridden tapestry. The corruption wasn't just a few crooked officials' funds–it was a network, sprawling and insidious, ensnaring law enforcement, business moguls, and even members of the governing council. The city's laws had become a plaything for those who could afford to twist them, and at the heart of it all, pulling unseen strings, was a name all of them had learned the hard way: Azareth.

Jorek slid a thick dossier onto the table, his past as an investigator for Eterna's Watch making him invaluable in tracking down the players involved. "We have plenty."

Sera's celestial aura dimmed slightly, her expression grim. "Forced servitude. Oaths taken not just in words but in flesh and soul. No wonder these people don't want to talk."

Cassian's claws flexed against the stone tabletop. "Then we make them talk."

Naomi gave him a pointed look. "We do this the right way. No tearing throats out."

Lucian, lounging against the far wall, smirked. "Shame. It'd be faster."

Veyra, ever the ghost in the room, spoke from the shadows. "Names. We need names."

The list was staggering. Names began surfacing, one after another. Councilor Draeven and Brionne were two of the most powerful voices in the city. They had been taking bribes, pushing policies that directly benefited Azareth's unseen hand. But they weren't alone.

Councilor Selrik Ashbourne was the Minister of Trade. The ledgers were riddled with discrepancies- shipments marked as 'spoiled goods' but actually carrying stolen relics and smuggled artifacts. He had worked alongside Lord Merrick for years, laundering money under the guise of 'economic development.'

Magistrate Evelyn Vaelor was the Head of Internal Security. It was her job to oversee investigations into corruption, yet her name appeared in dozens of records detailing political cover-ups. She had arranged 'accidents' for those who dug too deeply and silenced informants before they could speak.

General Hadrian Orlan was a name the whole team knew well. He was the Commander of Eterna's Guard. He had ignored crimes that benefited the elite, ensuring that influential figures remained untouchable. His own men were found listed in secret payrolls, paid off to overlook illegal activities.

Housekeepers, stewards, and advisors stood in nervous clusters, some shifting uncomfortably under the scrutiny. Naomi, Lucian, and Riven stood together. Cassian loomed nearby, his instincts on high alert as Rowan whispered quiet incantations under her breath, ensuring no illusion or deception clouded their findings. Sera's aura kept the room subdued, her presence a constant reminder that the righteous would always uncover the truth.

Jorek and Talon had been questioning the staff. "We've spoken with everyone," Talon said, flipping through his notes. "They're all accounted for—except one particular staff member, Lorien Vale. He was Merrick's steward, a high-ranking servant responsible for managing all his private affairs and schedules. According to the others, Lorien is a faeblood—half fae, half human—a rare lineage. This allows him to move between the mortal and fae realms. With a natural talent for concealment, Lorien could slip through shadows and remain unnoticed, which explains why no one has seen him since that fateful night. Merrick's personal guard also confirmed that Lorien was here the night of the murder but hasn't been seen since."

"Convenient, I'd say," Jorek muttered. The former investigator of Eterna's Watch had seen this before: a sudden disappearance usually meant either witness or involvement.

"Who was he last seen with?" Naomi asked

One of Merrick's chief advisors, a man named Elias Corvail, hesitated before speaking. "Councilor Draeven," he admitted in a shaky voice.

A heavy silence settled over the room. Naomi exchanged a glance with Riven. That was the break they had been looking for.

Sera frowned, her glow dimming with concern. "A witness in hiding. If he's still alive, he may have seen something."

Lucian's eyes gleamed as he considered the implications. "If he's been in hiding this whole time, he knows something dangerous."

It was Rowan who found the first trace of Lorien. Using a scrying spell, she detected residual fae energy deep within the manor's lower levels. She led the way, her torch casting flickering shadows that danced along the ancient corridor walls. The passageways, hidden beneath the manor, were unlike anything they had expected—more than simple cellars or storage chambers, they were winding, filled with forgotten relics and remnants of a past long buried.

Sera's celestial glow barely reached the ceiling, which arched high above them, reinforced with age-darkened wood and iron brackets. The deeper they went, the more oppressive the air became. Something was wrong here. Rowan ran a hand along the stone, eyes narrowed. "There's magic woven into these walls," she muttered. "Old magic. It's not just age making this place feel…unnatural."

Riven signaled for silence as they reached a fork in the passageway. He studied the footprints in the dust—most were old, but one set was recent. "Someone's been through here," he said. "And not long ago."

Veyra moved ahead, her form blending with the darkness, her footfalls utterly silent. She scanned the branching pathways, her fingers brushing the walls as she searched for hidden mechanisms. The manor above had been opulent, grand in its outward display of wealth, but below, it was a different story. The stonework was uneven, patched in places where sections had crumbled over the years. Chains still hung from rusted hooks in one of the side chambers, remnants of some forgotten use.

Cassian sniffed the air, his werewolf senses detecting something others could not. "There's someone down here. I can smell them. Faint, but recent.

Naomi nodded. "Keep moving. Stay alert."

The group pressed forward, the light revealing more of the underground. Old doors were lining the passage, some locked, others broken open long ago. The deeper they ventured, the more hallways seemed to twist in unnatural ways, as if the architecture itself had been designed to disorient intruders.

Lucian traced a clawed finger along a deep scratch in one of the door frames. "Something was down here before us. Something big." His voice was low, his eyes scanning for movement.

They reached an archway leading into a vast chamber, its vaulted ceiling lost to darkness. At the far end, a collapsed staircase led even deeper into the earth. The dust in this area had been disturbed recently, and a faint shimmer of residual magic lingered in the air.

Rowan stepped forward, chanting softly under her breath. The air rippled as her spell revealed traces of a cloaking enchantment–one designed to keep something hidden.

And that's when Veyra spotted it. "Over there," she whispered. Motioning to a section of the wall. It looked unremarkable at first, just another stretch of old stone. But when she reached out, her hand disappeared into it.

"A concealed passage," Lucian said. "He's in there."

Naomi wasted no time. "Cassian, with me. Riven, cover the exit."

Cassian lunged forward, slamming his shoulder into the illusionary wall. It rippled like water before shattering–and behind it, cowering against the far wall, was Lorien Vale.

His violet faeblood eyes went wide with fear, his pale skin coated in dust. He had been hiding for days, his usually neat clothing tattered. He scrambled back as Cassian blocked his escape, but Naomi raised a hand, her voice firm but calm.

"Lorien. We're not here to hurt you."

The faeblood trembled, his breath coming in ragged gasps. "You…you don't understand," he whispered. "You shouldn't have come here," Lorien struggled, "Please–please, I didn't do anything! I swear!"

Naomi stepped forward. "Lorien, we're not here to hurt you. We're investigating Merrick's murder."

Lorien hesitated but finally nodded. "I was here that night. I saw everything."

The team gathered around as Lorien recounted his story.

"I had just finished escorting Councilor Draeven out and was finishing up the night's ledgers when I heard something–a disturbance in the main hall. I knew Lord Merrick was meeting someone, but this… this was different. I crept to the upper balcony and hid behind the drapes. That's when I saw them."

He swallowed hard, his hands shaking. "A figure in robes, hooded and unnatural. I couldn't see its face, but its voice…It wasn't human. It was something ancient. And it was angry."

Sera's wings tensed. "What did it say?"

"They argued. Merrick accused the figure of breaking their agreement. He said he wouldn't be a part of it, that he had all the evidence he needed to expose everything. And then…" Lorien shuddered. "The figure raised a hand. Dark magic–no, something worse than magic–spread through the air. Merrick collapsed, lifeless, before he even hit the desk.

Riven's jaw clenched. "And then?"

"The figure pulled out a dagger and stabbed him in the chest. Then it turned, as if sensing someone else was there. I didn't breathe. I didn't move. I just… faded into the shadows. It searched, but it didn't see me. Then, after a few minutes, it vanished."

The room was silent as everyone processed the weight of Lorien's words.

Chapter 17

Hunting The Corrupt

The cold night air settled over Eterna like a shroud as Noami and her team made their way through the city's winding streets. Lorien, the witness they had extracted from Merrick Manor's lower level, had passed out and was slumped against Cassian's broad shoulder. The werewolf carried him with ease as the team moved swiftly toward their safe house– a repurposed warehouse close to Central Command.

Veyra scouted ahead, her form slipping in and out of the shadows like a ghost. Talon covered their rear, keeping his rifle ready in case anyone had taken an interest in their movements. Naomi and Riven walked in tandem, their minds already working through the next phase of the operation.

Inside the warehouse, the air was thick with the scent of oil and old wood. Newly delivered crates of weapons and supplies lined the walls, remnants of their previous missions stored for emergencies. Cassian deposited Lorien onto a cot, rolling his shoulders as he stepped back.

"Jorek, you're up," Naomi said, turning to the former investigator.

Jorek crossed his arms, watching the unconscious man with a calculating gaze. "I'll make sure he stays put. If he wakes up, I'll see if I can get anything else out of him and let you know. We'll stay put."

And with that, the team disappeared into the city, their mission clear–dismantle Azareth's network, one corrupt official at a time.

Councilor Draeven's estate loomed over the city's lower district, a decadent structure filled with stolen wealth. It was here that he and Brionne had orchestrated backroom deals, ensuring that the powerful remained untouched while the weak suffered. They had been instrumental in covering up Azareth's influence, silencing those who dared question their dealings.

Naomi led the charge, slipping past the guards at the gate with practiced ease. Rowan whispered an incantation under her breath, weaving a veil of silence around them as they moved through the corridors. Cassian and Talon took positions outside, ready to intercept any unwanted visitors.

Inside the council chamber, Draeven and Brionne sat over a table, documents spread before them. Their conversation was hushed but urgent, no doubt planning their next move now that Merrick's death had put their conspiracy at risk.

They never saw Naomi coming.

Within moments, the team had them restrained, their protests cut short by Riven's cold glare.

"You think you can just walk in here and–" Brionne started, but Naomi slammed a dagger into the table between them, silencing them.

"We're past that," she said. "You're going to tell us everything. And if you hold back, I promise you, Azareth's cult won't be the one you need to fear."

Draeven paled, eyes darting toward the windows as if searching for an escape. But there was none.

As the team extracted their confessions, it became clear that Draeven and Brionne had been key facilitators of Azareth's financial web. They had funneled money into ghost accounts, shifting funds through the Ministry of Trade, ensuring that illicit shipments arrived without scrutiny. Lord Merrick had discovered their scheme and had planned to expose them. That was why he was killed. But their influence had extended beyond money. They had connections, people in positions of power willing to do whatever was necessary to protect their conspiracy. And the next one on the list was one of those people.

The Ministry of Trade was the lifeblood of Eterna's economy, but under Selrik Ashbourne's control, it had become something else entirely—a front for Azareth's operations.

Selkirk was known for his smooth demeanor, a politician who had charmed his way into power. But beneath his facade was a man who had ensured that illegal shipments of weapons, arcane artifacts, and stolen goods flowed in and out of the city unchecked.

The team found him in his office, surrounded by ledgers and maps detailing the routes of contraband. He barely had time to register their presence before Rowan cast a binding spell, locking him in place.

"You've made a mistake," Selkirk hissed, his eyes darting to the door. "I have powerful allies–"

"And we've already dealt with two of them," Naomi interrupted. "You're next."

Selkirk's bravado crumbled when Riven threw a stack of documents onto his desk–proof of his involvement, his signatures sealing deals that had doomed innocent people. His silence spoke volumes.

He hadn't just helped Azareth–he had ensured that the city's resources were bent to his will. Trade agreements had been falsified, allowing forbidden artifacts to enter the city unchecked. Magic that should have been locked away had been sold to the highest bidder. And all of it led back to the true mastermind.

No corruption could flourish without protection, and that was where Evelyn Vaelor came in. As the head of internal security, she had been tasked with rooting out crime–yet she had been the one ensuring that investigations into Azareth's network went nowhere. Informants who got too close had vanished. Witnesses had been coerced into silence.

Naomi and her team stormed her residence, catching her in the act of burning documents in her fireplace. Lucian moved with vampiric speed, snatching her wrist before she could reach for her weapon.

"You've spent years hiding the truth," he murmured, his grip tightening. "That ends tonight."

Evelyn struggled, but she knew there was no escape. "You have no idea what you're up against," she said.

Cassian's snarl cut through the room. "We know exactly what we're up against. The only question is whether you want to cooperate or be left to the cult's mercy because Azareth is dead." Her silence confirmed what they had suspected. She feared the Ascendants cult more than she feared them.

General Hadron Orlin had been the city's shield, the man entrusted with keeping its streets safe. Instead, he had ignored the rot festering within its walls.. He had taken bribes, ensured the cult's shipments moved unchallenged, and used his power to silence dissenters.

Capturing him was no easy feat. His personal guards were well-trained, but they were no match for a team that had spent years dismantling threats far worse than a corrupt general.

When they finally had him in custody, Naomi leaned in close, her voice a whisper. "You knew everything, didn't you?" she asked.

Orlin sneered, even in chains. "I did what needed to be done. Eterna belongs to the strong."

"No, it belongs to those who fight for it. And you? You sold it piece by piece," Sera furiously said.

As they dragged him from his stronghold and hauled them all back to Central Command, Naomi knew that they were inching closer to uncovering the full extent of the cult's influence.

Jorek had pinned a city map to the wall of the safehouse command, marking locations tied to the corruption: warehouse, underground meeting places, political offices, the temple.

"It's everywhere," he said grimly.

Rowan crossed her arms. We're not dealing with corruption. We're dealing with an empire."

Riven's voice was quiet. "And we still don't know where the Ascendants are or exactly what the Herald's Decent Project is."

Naomi exhaled slowly, her fingers tightening around the edge of the table. "Then we keep pushing. We keep dragging people in. Everyone cracks eventually."

Cassian's smirk was all teeth. "Good. I'm getting tired of playing nice."

The web had been uncovered, its strands reaching higher than they'd dared imagine. But they weren't finished. The city was still sick, its infection running deep. And if Azareth and the Ascendants cult had gone unseen for so long, then they were more dangerous than any of them had realized.

The team still wasn't at the top. There were whispers of someone else. Someone even Azareth had answered to. They had more names. They had locations.

Now, they just needed to burn it all down.